The Besieged City

ALSO BY CLARICE LISPECTOR
AVAILABLE FROM NEW DIRECTIONS

THE BESIEGED CITY

Clarice Lispector

Translated from the Portuguese by Johnny Lorenz

Introduction by Benjamin Moser

Edited by Benjamin Moser

A NEW DIRECTIONS BOOK

First published clothbound by New Directions in 2019
Manufactured in the United States of America
New Directions Books are printed on acid-free paper
Design by Erik Rieselbach

Library of Congress Cataloging-in-Publication Data
Names: Lispector, Clarice, author. | Lorenz, Johnny, translator. |
Moser, Benjamin, editor
Title: The besieged city / by Clarice Lispector ; translated by Johnny Lorenz ;
edited by Benjamin Moser.
Other titles: Cidade sitiada. English
Description: New York : New Directions, 2019. | Originally published
as A Cidade Sitiada in 1949.
Identifiers: LCCN 2018046582 (print) | LCCN 2018059175 (ebook) |
ISBN 9780811226721 (ebook) | ISBN 9780811226714 (alk. paper)
Classification: LCC PQ9697.L585 (ebook) | LCC PQ9697.L585 C513 2019 (print) |
DDC 869.3/42—dc23
LC record available at https://lccn.loc.gov/2017051736

10 9 8 7 6 5 4 3 2 1

New Directions Books are published for James Laughlin
by New Directions Publishing Corporation
80 Eighth Avenue, New York 10011

Contents

Explicam-se as emendas abaixo com a impossibilidade da autora, residindo então na Suíça, assistir e acompanhar a confecção gráfica do livro. Regressando ao país quando o livro já se encontrava impresso, e reconhecida como indispensável a necessidade de reformar certos detalhes, êstes ficam aqui registrados:

Pág.	Linha(s)	Onde se lê:	Leia-se:
7	18	em náuseas e ofuscamento.	em náusea e ofuscamento
25	15	a dos são-geraldenses — e ao mesmo tempo	a dos são-geraldenses — ao mesmo tempo
25	25	Por um instante uma cara de alcance	Por um instante uma cara fora de alcance
33	14 a 16	De uma balaustrada superior êles viram uma velha de guarda-sol aberto na outra balaustrada — o subúrbio subindo e descendo em escadas de penitenciária.	De uma balaustrada de ferro podia-se ver a praça ao longe. Mas de uma balaustrada superior êles viram uma velha de guarda-sol aberto na outra balaustrada — o subúrbio subindo e descendo em escadas de penitenciária.
33	26	bruço	busto
48	28	Com um piano	Como um piano
71	28	sonhava com liberdade como uma guerra.	sonhava com liberdade como numa guerra.
89	8 e 9	mas tudo era castanho. Durante o relento	mas tudo era castanho. As manhãs eram úmidas em S. Geraldo. Durante o relento
95	7	então me perguntava	então me perguntavam
110	36	pois era masculino e misterioso!	pois era tão masculino e misterioso!
132	31	nem a levara ao amor por si próprio.	nem a levara ao amor por si própria.
134	38	sobrevivendo com obscura vitória.	sobrevivendo como obscura vitória.
135	21	a dizer que fôra para sempre ferida,	a dizer que fôra ferida,
153	35-36	Bom! que não precisasse explicar onde estivera	Bom que não precisasse explicar onde estivera
160	9	Esquecendo-se cada vez mais.	Esquecendo-o cada vez mais.

Obyezloshadenie

IN 1920, AT THE TIME OF CHAYA PINKHASOVNA LISPEC-tor's birth in a Ukrainian village, Isaac Babel—born just down the road a generation earlier—was traveling with the Bolshevik army. He was chronicling the horrors of the war, including the anti-Semitic pogroms that caused Chaya's family to flee. As he followed the cavalry, he was also chronicling the travails of the animal that, for millennia, had accompanied every aspect of human work and warfare. Now, that indispensable creature was gradually being replaced by motors. Babel named the process *obyezloshadenie*.

Twenty-five years later, "dehorsification" would provide the most poignant metaphor in a book Chaya—by then a Brazilian named Clarice—was writing. *The Besieged City* tells of a girl's transformation into a woman, and a township's transformation into a city. The settlement's "civilization" makes its formerly humble denizens slick and chatty; and as São Geraldo expands, words, possessions, and marriage progressively dehorse Lucrécia. She is grateful to be domesticated—but the animals retreat, and *The Besieged City* ends with their surrender: "the last horses had already emigrated, surrendering the metropolis to the glory of its mechanism."

In 1971, Clarice Lispector told an interviewer to read *The Besieged City*—"if you manage," she shrugged."Even I thought it was hard." Elsewhere she referred to her third novel as "one of my least liked books," and professed her own bafflement with the story of the girl from São Geraldo.

Every educated Brazilian knows G. H. and Macabéa. But only the devoted *clariceano* will quickly recognize the name of Lucrécia Neves Correia. In a country groaning beneath the weight of writings on Clarice Lispector, the book of which Lucrécia is the protagonist is an orphan. Essays and articles about it, in Brazil, are rare, and it seems to be little-read. Sales indicate that it is the least popular of her novels.

The book nearly killed her career. She became famous with her first novel, *Near to the Wild Heart*, published when she was twenty-three. Her second, *The Chandelier*, published three years later, in 1946, was less successful, although—more likely because—it is even more ambitious than her first. She finished *The Chandelier* in Naples, where she was accompanying her husband, the young Brazilian diplomat Maury Gurgel Valente. They arrived with the war raging—Clarice nursed wounded Brazilian soldiers; Maury helped reestablish the foreign service—but this dramatic start to their overseas careers ended with the Allied victory. In 1946, they were posted to Bern, the capital of a country untouched by the war. The contrast with Naples was glaring.

"The city lacks a demon," she wrote a friend.

Boredom and exile sharpened the depression she already suffered before her marriage, and which her wartime activities kept at bay. Now, all she had to do was go to the movies, take sculpture class, and learn how to knit—though she drew the line at playing cards.

"This Switzerland," she wrote her sister, "is a cemetery of sensations."

She hated being away from her friends, her family, and her country. "It's bad to be away from the land where you grew up," she told another friend. "It's horrible to hear foreign languages all around you, everything seems rootless."

For all that, Bern had two saving graces, gestating simultaneously: her first child, and *The Besieged City*. "My gratitude to that book is enormous: the effort of writing it kept me busy, saved me from the appalling silence of Bern, and when I finished the last chapter I went to the hospital to give birth to the boy."

The book was rejected by the publisher of *The Chandelier*. She asked her sister to help, warning her not to read it. "It is so tiresome, really. And you might suffer by having to tell me that you don't like it and feel bad about seeing me literally lost."

More rejections followed. When, at last, a publisher accepted it, reviewers who had expressed excitement about her previous work scratched their heads.

"It's a dense, closed book," she wrote. "I was chasing after something and there was nobody to tell me what it was."

Few tried.

"Its hermeticism has the texture of the hermeticism of dreams," a critic said. "May someone find the key."

*

In the early part of this century, I began amassing materials for my biography of Clarice Lispector. "The early part of this century" was less than two decades ago. But technological changes created such a gulf between then and now that the phrase seems warranted: it was, for example, just before the digital camera made it possible to photograph as much as one wanted of virtually anything; and I can still see myself sitting in the archive, pencil in hand, copying out letters, word by arduous word.

"The early part of this century" was also just before most booksellers went online. It was unthinkable, when I set out, to have millions of books available with a click. Since I neither lived in Brazil nor in a place with an outstanding Brazilian research collection, I did not see any alternative but to build a library of my own. Finding books was a great labor. I vainly chased citations—even hints of citations—up and down the country. On my visits, there was never enough time to find them all.

I feel no nostalgia for note-taking. But I've never given up prowling for books. I earned a knowledge of the Brazilian bibliography impossible to acquire without those thousands of apparently fruitless hours. And every researcher knows that finding something you're not looking for is very often more exciting than finding something you are. Precisely because the internet makes it easy to find what you're looking for, it can make it harder to find the things you're not.

When they became available, the databases confirmed my intuition that certain books—cheap and popular in appearance—are, in fact, surpassingly rare. A paperback novel published in 1964 might cost pennies when you find it; but precisely because it was cheap and popular nobody cherished it, and almost every copy got put out with the trash.

I still collect Brazilian books because objects need curators, explicators. Every bibliophile has seen the mysterious way in which books magnify books, and fragments communicate with fragments. Books, like people, exist most happily in society.

*

Several years ago, I came across a first edition of *The Besieged City*. Printed on brittle, acidic paper, not widely read or reviewed at the time of publication, this book has nonetheless survived in many copies, making it the most common early edition of Clarice Lispector. I had one. I would probably not have bought another—except for a single-page insert that I had never seen, and have never encountered since.

It reads:

> The following changes are explained by the impossibility of the author, then residing in Switzerland, to be present for the typesetting of the book. Returning to the country when the book was already printed, and recognizing as indispensible the need to correct certain details, they follow below.

The fifteen amendments include single-letter typos—"com" (with) versus "como" (how); "sonhava com liberdade como uma guerra" (she was dreaming freely like a war) versus "sonhava com liberdade como numa guerra" (she was dreaming freely as in a war)—that would escape even an attentive eye, particularly one accustomed to this writer's arabesques. The revisions change nothing for the reader. But they were important enough for the writer to go to the trouble to have the page printed, and included in the book.

The commercial value of this leaf is zero. The prose it contains, the paragraph above, is bureaucratic—even, with that dangling participle, ungrammatical. Yet it becomes intriguing when seen alongside another discovery I made when I had already edited a full draft of this translation. When arranging some books on my shelves, I happened upon a sorry-looking second edition. It had turned up at auction a decade ago, signed by Clarice Lispector. Such signed copies are rare, but this one was in bad shape—a paperback, stripped of its cover; a second edition, not a first—and not dedicated to anyone famous ("Rosa"). It was not expensive.

Now, I noticed a word, "revista," revised, that I had not noticed before, and had never spotted on any other edition of Clarice's works. Because I was already deep into this work, I decided to see what she had revised. Editing these books means taking them through several drafts, an unbearably tedious process that also happens to be indispensible. If I had not happened to be in the middle of that sculpting already, I would never have voluntarily put a second edition under this microscopic lens.

Yet as I did, I found modifications on every page: hundreds in all. I tried to find another copy to send to the translator. Online, there was nothing. But as I worked through the draft, I saw that to consider this second edition alongside the first and the errata was to see something extraordinary. The three documents, taken together, showed nothing less than a manuscript of Clarice Lispector's writing in process.

*

Such a manuscript has long been a scholarly grail. With the exception of *Água Viva*, which exists in two versions, and some works left unfinished at her death, her drafts do not exist. They must have, at some point: she claimed to have rewritten *The Apple in the Dark* eleven times. But none of these versions have survived. In any case, she claimed never to revise or reread published work. "When I reread what I've written," she said to a friend, "I feel like I'm swallowing my own vomit."

As she came into maturity, her writing came to recall poetry as Wordsworth defined it, "the spontaneous overflow of powerful feelings." The appearance of spontaneous overflow was a hallmark of her style. Like Frans Hals or Vincent van Gogh, she seemed to be an action painter; she wrote, rumor would later have it, in a trance. But to see these revisions is to discover—as when viewing a painting with x-rays—that beneath the furious surface lurks a deliberate and painstaking architecture.

To see these several stages is to see how much, and for how long, *The Besieged City* obsessed her. She began it in 1946; the second edition dates to 1964. This means that, in some form or another, she was working on this book for eighteen years. Even when she was still in Bern, her protracted rewriting shocked her housekeeper. It was better to be a cook than a writer, the woman told her employer—since "if you put too much salt in the food, there's nothing you can do about it."

Clarice wrote her sister:

> I'm struggling with the book, which is horrible. How did I find the courage to publish the other two? I don't know how to forgive the thoughtlessness of writing. But I've already based myself entirely on writing and if that desire goes, there won't be anything left. So that's the way it has to be. But I've reached the conclusion that writing is what I want more than anything else in the world, even more than love.

Her letters from Switzerland show she was severely depressed; it may not be too much to say that, with this book, her life was on the line. Was that why it was so hard to let go? When she did, she was embarrassed that she clung to it so ardently. The claim on the errata that she had not overseen its publication is untrue, for example: she was in Rio for several months before the book came out, and never returned to Switzerland.

In the second edition, she cleans up some grammar: the last sentence of Chapter 4, in the first edition, could refer either to Lucrécia or to the living room; the second edition resolves this. She changes pronouns to names—"Lucrécia" instead of "she"—or replaces the neutral pronoun with something explicit: "An instant when one would express oneself" becomes "An instant when she'd express herself." She minimizes the passive voice: "resistance itself would have been broken so often before" becomes "she'd have so often before broken resistance itself."

This is tidying: copyediting. Elsewhere, she inserts the word "já" (now, already), a quickening additional syllable. She adds: beginning Chapter 5 with "A bit later," for example. She explains: "she rubbed the railing with her sleeve" becomes "she rubbed the railing of the Library with her sleeve." In the same chapter, she eliminates "like telegram signals." And in Chapter 7, she even strikes a sentence—"The mornings were humid in São Geraldo"—that she had inserted in the errata.

*

The most significant changes have the effect of cracking a window, opening a door. Throughout, she breaks up the long black blocs of the first edition, splitting paragraphs into five, six, and even seven separate sections. This extra white space allows the reader to move down the page with far greater ease.

Stranger is the punctuation. Breaking rhythms, adding pauses, shifting emphases, hundreds of commas are sprinkled throughout, changing the music of her prose, clarifying difficult passages—and then, just as often, muddying them further, weird little hairs in the soup. She changes some passages. Others, exactly comparable, she stets.

Yet there is nothing offhand about her punctuation. "My punctuation is my breath," she said. In the 1950s, she haughtily ordered the French publisher of *Near to the Wild Heart* to lay off her commas: "You will agree that the elementary principles of punctuation are taught in every school." At the end of the 1960s, when she began writing for the Rio newspaper *Jornal do Brasil*, she impressed upon her editor, over and over again, that the young woman was not to disturb "so much as a comma."

The theme crops up constantly. This insistence, and the attention she paid to *The Besieged City* over nearly two decades, makes the changes she chose not to make as noteworthy as those she did. The longer one studies them, the more cryptic they come to seem. One can only conclude that this mystery was at least partially the point. In November 1958, an editor wrote to invite her to contribute to a new magazine: "We would like to read your stories which we never considered *intelligible*."

The appeal was well-phrased. She sent the stories.

*

One challenge of translating *The Besieged City* is its range of "vision words": *divisar, encarar, enxergar, espiar, fitar, observar, olhar, parecer, perceber, pressentir, prever, rever, sentir, ver, vigiar*. With all their aspects, in all the idioms they populate, embroidered by Clarice Lispector's poetic usages, they describe nuances of seeing. Sometimes Lucrécia looks or sees instead of saying or thinking: "This city is mine, the woman looked." Sometimes these words are used in ways that are hard to understand.

Yet if the language can be inscrutable, there is nothing unintelligible about Lucrécia Neves. Unlike the protagonists of Clarice's first two novels, Lucrécia is vain and pretentious, content to remain on the surface. Lucrécia—there it is in her name—is lucre, just another one of the porcelain knickknacks in her mother's sitting room: "Behold, behold, all of her, terribly physical, one of the objects." Her ambitions are material, and she is the most insolently superficial woman Clarice ever portrayed.

But another way to read Lucrécia's "objectification" appears when placed alongside Simone de Beauvoir's *The Second Sex*, also published in 1949. This book, too, shows how women see and are seen. Beauvoir understands human relations as a battle of gazes, and the battle between men and woman is fought between one who looks and one who is looked at; subject and object; master and slave. The male gaze is the default, to which women must adapt. Male pronouns are universal: "man" encompasses woman but "woman" does not encompass man. Man is the first sex. Woman is the second.

Woman therefore "becomes an object; and she grasps herself as an object," Beauvoir writes. "Once she has accepted her vocation as sex object, she enjoys adorning herself." This is the objectification—particularly Lucrécia's tacky, frivolous savoring of it—that Clarice Lispector ironizes. Lucrécia lacks the fire, the rebelliousness, of the girls in Clarice's early stories. Instead, like the objectified women Beauvoir describes, she endeavors to make herself into a thing—and succeeds.

To do so, a woman must discern, distinguish, foresee, look, observe, perceive, see, seem, spy, watch. Her tool in this underground work is the mirror, which, properly employed, will help her turn herself into an ideal—a shiny object, a public statue. In the mirror, she contemplates "her marvelous double," Beauvoir writes: "the promise of happiness, a work of art, a living statue." Lucrécia is "a statue at whose feet, during civic festivals, flowers would be placed," and who aspires to be a faceless Greek fragment: "Dreaming of being Greek was the only way not to scandalize oneself."

At first, Lucrécia, like the horses, kicks; she, too, has hooves. Through contemplating herself at the mirror and cannily adapting to its demands, she is dehorsed. Marriage completes the task begun in girlhood: "The recently married woman felt it had been years since she'd seen a cow or a horse."

*

After the second edition of 1964, Clarice would not muck with the text again. But she never spoke of any of her books as insistently as she spoke of this one. She often mentioned it in interviews. "I was pleasantly surprised to learn that some people who had read *The Besieged City* and who hadn't liked or understood it on their first reading, identified more with the work when they reread it," she said in 1960. In 1970, she wondered, in response to an unnamed critic's incomprehension: "Does this mean I couldn't bring to the fore the book's intentions?"

In *A Breath of Life*, the great work left unfinished at her death, Clarice Lispector returned one last time to this book. The writings she produced in the three decades since she began *The Besieged City* unfolded numinous meanings that are only latent—subjacent—here. They provide the key that was missing at the time of publication. A retrospective knowledge of Clarice Lispector's work shows that Lucrécia's thing-ness is not merely sexual, or sociological: it represents the mystery of the creation, by God, of the being—and the creation, by the being, of the thing.

"The object—the thing—always fascinated me and in a certain sense destroyed me. In my book *The Besieged City* I speak indirectly about the mystery of the thing. The thing is a specialized and immobilized animal," she wrote in *A Breath of Life*. The word "thing" acquires layer upon layer of resonance in Clarice's work, and comes, finally, to represent an aspiration, both linguistic and spiritual. "People speak, or rather, used to speak so much about my 'words,' about my 'phrases,'" she wrote of this book. "As if they were verbal. Yet not one, not a single one, of the words in the book was—a game. Each of them essentially meant some thing."

The objectification of Lucrécia is a warning, as it would have been for Simone de Beauvoir. But it is also a kind of terrifying ideal. "What did I mean to say through Lucrécia—a character without the weapons of intelligence, who aspires, nonetheless, to that kind of spiritual integrity of a horse, who doesn't 'share' what it sees, who has no mental or 'vocabular vision' of things," Clarice wrote in her answer to the critic in 1970. Lucrécia's desire to escape from language connects her to other figures in Clarice's work, from Virgínia in *The Chandelier* to Martim in *The Apple in the Dark* to G. H. in *The Passion According to G. H.* In that book, Clarice reveals the full horror of stripping away everything a person sees in a mirror: false personality; clichéd, received language; all the sticky deposits that gather on our animal soul, and give it, for ourselves and for others, an intelligible form.

It may seem ironic that any writer should seek to escape the "vocabular vision." But Clarice Lispector was a mystic. That is why Lucrécia's identification with the horses is so revealing, and fraught. She tries to drown wordlessness, "that feels no need to complete impression with expression," with babble. As she does, she estranges herself from the perfect language, the language beyond words, "beyond thought." The Greek word for horse is *álogo*—"unreasoning, without speech." Could becoming a Greek horse be the only way to avoid scandalizing oneself?

*

Yet the struggle against objectification in the concrete, sociological, Beauvoirian sense—the struggle between intelligibility and unintelligibility—is present in this book too. The incomprehension that greeted this book had serious, nearly fatal, consequences for her career. Her next novel was rejected, year after demoralizing year, by every good publisher in Brazil—and by lots of bad ones, too. *The Apple in the Dark* would only come out in 1961, twelve years after *The Besieged City*.

Clarice spent the fifties in Chevy Chase, in the Washington suburbs. Far from home, unable to publish, struggling with one of her sons' mental illness, she was also trapped in a marriage that, while unsatisfying, was not abusive or particularly miserable. Indeed, it offered advantages: a partner who loved her, stability for her children, financial freedom to pursue her writing. Marriage also allowed her to avoid the stigma that, in those days, attached to any Brazilian woman who left her husband.

Yet the battle did not relent between the diplomatic spouse—by all accounts she was exceptionally capable—and the creature "straight from the zoo" that explodes from her early books. She was tormented by awareness of the phoniness into which her husband's role pressed her. "I remembered a time in which I arrived at the refinement (!?) of having the waiter at home pass fingerbowls to all the guests in the following way: every fingerbowl had a rose petal floating in the liquid," she wrote.

Already in Switzerland, she was taking barbiturates. Throughout her years abroad, she struggled against what Sartre and Beauvoir called "bad faith"—the temptation to slide into anesthesia. The woman who makes herself an object was one of the three types of woman that Beauvoir catalogued as acting in bad faith; but the existentialists, who had seen the agonizing conflicts that arose under Nazi occupation, knew that the calculations leading to bad faith were not flippantly made.

Surrender, for many people, was a matter of life and death. It could be lavishly rewarded—and not only in the form of the hotels and haberdashers to which Lucrécia, following her marriage, ascends. The choice between Clarice Lispector and Clarice Gurgel Valente was not one that could be swiftly resolved. Beauvoir nonetheless insisted that a woman must choose freedom over the tawdry temptation of happiness.

The Besieged City was written amidst this struggle. This may be why, for every passage she clarified in her revisions, she left another rough—sometimes roughed it up more. To go through it carefully is to see passages as grammatically gristly as anything this difficult writer ever wrote. To see everything she left unexplained is to see her resistance to the reflexive—to see her wavering between good faith and bad.

Good faith meant commercial failure and critical befuddlement, the end of her marriage and the breakup of her family.

But Clarice Lispector was not resigned to *obyezloshadenie*. In 1959, she left her husband and returned with her two sons to Rio de Janeiro. Then, in 1964, the year of the second edition of *The Besieged City*, she published *The Passion According to G. H.* It made no concessions. The horses were back.

BENJAMIN MOSER
LES EYZIES-DE-TAYAC, SEPTEMBER 2018

xxi

The Besieged City

In heaven, learning is seeing;
On earth, remembering.

—Pindar

1   *The Hill in the Pasture*

"ELEVEN O'CLOCK," SAID LIEUTENANT FELIPE.

He'd barely spoken when the church bells struck their first chime, golden, solemn. The people seemed to hear space for a moment ... the banner in an angel's hand froze trembling. But suddenly the fireworks rose and exploded amidst the chimes. The crowd, roused from the sudden sleepiness to which they had succumbed, abruptly started moving and once again cries burst out on the carousel.

Above the heads the lanterns were misting up quivering the vision; the fair stalls were warping as they dripped. When Felipe and Lucrécia reached the Ferris wheel the bell shook above the night filling the religious festival with emotion— the movement of the crowd became more anxious and freer. The population had flocked to celebrate the township and its saint, and in the dark the courtyard of the church was shining. Mixing with the burnt gunpowder the blackcurrant drink was lifting faces in nausea and darkening. Faces were appearing, disappearing. Lucrécia found herself so close to a face that it laughed at her. It was hard to notice that it was laughing at someone lost in the shadows. The girl also pretended to talk to Felipe, looking however into a stranger's eyes that were filled by the brightness of a streetlamp: what a night! she said to the stranger, and the two faces hesitated: the carrousel was illuminating the air in twirls, the lights falling trembling ... If any extraordinary thing were finally to happen in the township, it would come bursting into range of the military band, where children were wandering away from their mothers and shouting would be just another shout: the church square was fragile. And crackling with the chestnuts on the bonfire. Drowsy, stubborn, people were elbowing one other until joining the silent circle that had formed around the flames.

Once beside the fire, they'd stop and watch, reddened.

The flames were sharpening gestures, the enormous heads moving about mechanical, smooth. Some components of the afternoon procession, still in silky, tight clothes, were mingling with the spectators. Crowned with cardboard a sleepless girl was shaking her curls—it was Saturday night. Beneath her hat Lucrécia's dimly lit face sometimes looked delicate, sometimes monstrous. She was peeking out. Her face had a sweet watchfulness, without malice, her dark eyes peeking at the fire's mutations, her hat with the flower.

Once again dragged along by Felipe, they were now heading in an unknown direction through the crowd, pushing, feeling their way. Lucrécia was smiling with satisfaction. Her face wanted to advance but her body could barely go ahead because the festival was suddenly crammed, swept by a faraway initial contraction. She tried at least to free one of her hands and straighten her hat that dislodged over one eye was giving her happy face an expression of disaster. But Felipe was clasping her by the elbow protecting her and laughing ...

The lieutenant was raising his head above the others and laughing to the heavens.

The girl could hardly stand this free laughter that was an outsider's way of denigrating the poor festivity of São Geraldo. Though she herself couldn't fully dive into the center of the jubilation that sometimes would seem to crackle in the silence of the fire, sometimes whiz with the turns of the little horses— though she sought with her face the place from which the pleasure was gushing. Where could the center of a township be? Felipe was wearing his uniform. With the pretext of leaning against him the girl, blind, watchful, was running her fingers over the thick buttons. Suddenly they found themselves outside the festival.

They were in the almost-dark void because the people were cramming into the zone around the military band as if into a marked-off circle. From outside it really was strange to watch the inhabitants pressing into one another: the ones whose backs were already turned toward the void were struggling sleepwalking to get in. The young man and the girl were watching while shaking the dust from their clothes. Right then the bells in the tower struck faraway, peaceful ... The church bells shook more forcefully, mingling with the delicateness of the other hours. Lucrécia got worried. Before long, the lieutenant barely able to keep up with her, the girl was moving ahead almost running. The main event of the night in São Geraldo hadn't even been announced, the small town was miraculously intact still—Felipe was laughing irritated: don't run, girl! they turned the corner and found themselves in the square paved with stones. The clock tower was still trembling.

The plaza was naked. So unrecognizable in the moonlight that the girl didn't recognize herself. Felipe too had halted relieved: damned people! he exclaimed pushing back his kepi. Saturday was the night of several worlds: the lieutenant coughed transmitting to one after the next his wordless voice. The windows trembled at the neighing. There was no wind blowing. Despite the moon the statue of the horse in darkness. You could see, only a bit more distinctly, the tip of the horseman's sword suspending halted fire. The moonlight had stamped the thousand mute doors on the doors. And the square had been astonished into the crooked posture in which it had been touched. It was the same cold recognition as when you'd hear a blind man's clarinet … The flagstones almost revealed, you could barely touch them with your boots. The girl even clapped two hands … Which separated immediately into a deaf salute—the whole square was applauding. In less than a second the palms broke apart and the odd bit of applause was snuffed out in the alleys undefined by the darkness. The girl listened a bit hostile, her two hands finally pushed her hat down decisively on her head. She said goodbye to Felipe telling him it wasn't fitting to be seen together.

She'd just started walking by herself and was already regretting it because that was exactly what São Geraldo wanted. She was walking restrained, mechanical, even attempting a certain irony. But her steps were multiplying and the stone square was marching. She stopped without warning, tied the laces of her boot … When she raised her head she decided not to forget to look at the narrowest house, the smallest shadow. The closed shops with their rolling gates of iron. She was being gentle with all of them. I'm really touching this lamppost, she thought with more confidence. The lamppost was freezing.

Moments later the music from the bandstand was brought by the air—the band was proliferating beneath the yellow lights. But the sound was holding back at the edge of the deserted streets. Lucrécia looked up too, with a bit of insolence.

But in each window of the deserted city a man was swaying in the shadow of the blinds—the blinds were swinging. The young lady was trembling from fear of being alive. Certain things were giving the same sign—the lack of wind—a blind man playing an instrument—the moonlight on the stone ... she quickly made the sign of the cross while a fat rat was sunning himself beneath the lamppost. Dry steps rang out. The soldier diminished by the distance appeared on one corner and disappeared on another ... Saturday was the night for drunkards. A piece of paper was trembling on the ground: then she started to run before everything could start until she leaned against the door of her house. She pressed hard on the doorbell ...

The unexpected stridence of the sound was crossing the dark space. The girl seemed to have rung the bell of another city. She waited a moment. But after having made her presence known with the doorbell she no longer dared keep her back turned: she started knocking with closed fists, the rat was running peacefully by the sleeping wagon; she was knocking and looking to the sky—the transported clouds seeming motionless and the moon passing by ... she was knocking—knocking with closed fists looking at the sky, her hair growing longer in artlessness and horror, it was getting more and more dangerous, the houses upright ... Finally from the top of the stairs they pulled the cord connected to the lock. With a creak the door was opening.

Then the bells suddenly shook in glass, scattered from the band over the city, fireworks exploded. Things were breaking in disaster almost before she could take shelter—she shut the door hard.

Little by little, in the calming darkness, she let down her

guard. She was still bristling, each tip that went back to being a thing couldn't be touched, the twisted columns of the handrails. Also the size of São Geraldo had widened and she saw from bottom to top—the immense stairway to climb. The bells were ringing. Dlin, dlen, dlin, dlen, she heard with attention. She imagined that the streets must have all lit up to the sound of the bells ... The night now was golden. Lucrécia Neves had escaped.

The house where she lived was pierced with pipes and windows, which made it very weak—the girl was going up the steps that were trembling with the final vibrations of the bells.

The township of São Geraldo, in the year 192..., was already mingling some progress with the smell of the stable. The more factories that opened on the outskirts, the more the township arose to its own life without the inhabitants' being able to say what transformation was reaching them. Movements had already grown congested and you could no longer cross a street without dodging a wagon that the sluggish horses were pulling, while an impatient automobile was honking behind it spewing smoke. Even the twilights were now smoky and bloody. In the morning, amidst the trucks that were making their way to the new power plant, transporting wood and iron, baskets of fish were spread out on the sidewalk, arriving through the night from larger centers. From the houses disheveled women were coming down with pans, the fish were weighed almost by hand, while vendors in shirtsleeves were shouting out prices. And when above the happy morning movement the fresh and disturbing wind would blow, you'd think the whole population was getting ready for a journey.

At sunset invisible roosters would still crow. And mingling with the metallic dust of the factories the smell of the cows would nourish the dusk. But at night, with the streets suddenly deserted, you could already breathe in the silence with uneasiness, as in a city; and on the upper floors blinking with light everyone seemed to be seated. The nights would smell of manure and were cool. Sometimes it would rain.

The tumultuous life of Market Street was out of place in those surroundings where an old-fashioned taste reigned over the wrought-iron balconies, over the flat facades of the houses. And in the little church whose modest architecture had been erected in the old silence. Slowly, however, the stone square got lost amidst the cries with which the cart-drivers would imitate the animals in order to talk to them. Due to the increasingly urgent need for transport, waves of horses had invaded the township, and in the still-rustic children the secret desire to gallop was being born. A bay colt had even given a boy a deadly kick. And the place where the daring child had died was looked at by people with a reproach that they didn't really know where to direct.

With their baskets under their arms they would stop and look around.

Until a newspaper found out about the matter and with a certain pride an article was read—in which there was no lack of irony about the slowness with which a number of townships were becoming civilized—with the title of: "The Crime of the Horse in a Township."

This was the first clear name in São Geraldo, and someone finally being called, the residents were looking with resentment and admiration at the big animals that were invading the flat city at a trot. And that would suddenly halt with a long neigh, hooves upon the ruins. Inhaling with wild nostrils as if they'd known another era in their blood.

But at two in the afternoon the streets would grow dry and almost deserted, the sun instead of revealing things would hide them with light: the sidewalks were stretching indefinitely and São Geraldo was becoming a big city. Three stone women were holding up the portico of the modernist building still obstructed by some scaffolding: it was the only place with shade. A man had posted himself underneath. Ah! a bird was saying cutting sidelong the intense light. In reply the three women were holding up the building. Ah! the bird was crying while moving off over the rooftops. A dog was sniffing the sunlit sewers. Widely spaced men — card-players in straw hats with toothpicks in their mouths — were watching. A black face with white eyes came out of Iron Crown Charcoal Works. Lucrécia Neves stuck her head into the coolness of the charcoal works; she looked around a bit. When she drew it back — there was the sidewalk … Such reality, the girl was seeing. Each thing. She twisted her head as a way of looking. Each thing. But suddenly, in the silence of the sun, a team of horses ran out from a corner. For a moment they froze with raised hooves. Sparkling at their mouths.

Everyone watched from their posts, hard, separated.

Once the dazzle of the apparition had passed the horses curved their necks, lowered their hooves — the vagrants in straw hats moved off quickly, a window slammed shut. Reactivated Lucrécia entered the store.

When she left with her packages, the streets had already been transformed. Instead of the emptiness of the sun each thing was moving along the path of its own forms utilizing the slightest shadows. The township was now insignificant and painstaking: the afternoon had begun. Wherever there was water, the breeze was ruffling it. Iron shutters rolled up with the first jangling and the variety shop was revealed: the shop of things. The older an object, the more denuded it became. The form forgotten during its use was rising now in the shop window for the incomprehension of eyes—and that's how the girl was watching, coveting the little box of pink china.

There were two flowers painted on the lid.

Until the shadow of the mango tree stretched across the sidewalk. Once it reached that point the afternoon became immutable. Some folks thought about a picnic. But they didn't get around to it: one stayed standing on the corner—another was looking through the curtain of a window—another counted the stitches of her needlepoint one more time.

On that same day, when the sun was about to set, gold spread over clouds and over stones. The inhabitants' faces became golden like armor and that's how their rumpled hair was shining. Dusty factories were whistling continually, the wagon wheel gained a halo. In that pale gold in the breeze was an ascension of an unsheathed sword—that's how the statue in the square was rising. Passing through the streets more softly the men in the light seemed to come from the horizon and not from work. The township of charcoal and iron had transported itself to the top of a hill, the branches of the almond trees were swaying. Horses, the black earth and the dry cistern in the square had lent a certain arrogance to the residents of São Geraldo. And a boldness that recalled anger without rage. The men would often say to one another: what's up! don't you recognize me! it was common to have eyes gray and shining like plaques.

On Sunday morning the air would smell of steel and the dogs would bark at people leaving Mass. And in the afternoon, in the first anxieties of a city Sunday, the clean people on the street would look up: in a house someone was practicing the saxophone. They'd listen. As in a city, they already didn't know where to go.

Despite the progress the township retained almost deserted places, right on the border of the countryside. These places soon took the name of "promenades." And there were also people who, invisible in the former life, were now gaining a certain importance simply for refusing the new age. Old Efigênia lived an hour's walk past the Gate. When her husband had died she'd kept up the small corral, not wanting to get mixed up with the nascent sin. And though she only went to Market Street to deposit her milk bottles, she'd become a bit the boss of São Geraldo. She'd stop by a store, with her dry gaze that didn't seem to need to see, they'd ask her laughing from embarrassment how things were going, as if she could know more than everyone else. Since from São Geraldo's own development a timid desire for spirituality had been born, of which the A.F.Y.S.G. was one of the results. When Efigênia would say she awoke at dawn, she created great unease in the merchants who, in their capacity as employers, were already starting to say: São Geraldo needs a guideline. Though the spiritual life they'd vaguely attribute to Efigênia seemed to boil down to her neither agreeing or disagreeing, in not getting caught up even in herself, her austerity had reached that point. Of being silent and severe as happened to people who'd never had to think. Whereas in São Geraldo people were starting to talk a lot.

It was at that time of breeze and indecision, at that moment of a still barely built city, when the wind is an omen and the moonlight horrifies with its sign—it was in the clearing of this new age that the Association of Feminine Youth of São Geraldo was born and died. Initially devoted to charity, the group—whipped up by the engines of the power plant, interrupted by the traffic of the horses and by the sudden whistles of the factories—unexpectedly came to have its own anthem, and in a turnaround that frightened even the members—its aim was now that of ennobling beautiful things. The Association would have perhaps stuck to organizing raffles and recreational activities if not for Cristina who would light a fire that was void and destined for the void, in which the members would be consumed in the name of the soul that must progress. Gradually the young women would gather with an ardor that in fact already had no cause. In the afternoon you'd see entering the meetinghouse hurried groups of small young women, with low hips and long hair, the feminine type of that area. In the name of an already frightening hope they'd spur themselves on and express themselves in the anthem that spoke with barely contained violence of the joy of flowers, Sundays and goodness. They were afraid of the city that was being born. On the sung Sundays they would sew, at noon breaking off suffocated, running their hands over their lips that soft hair would darken; they went to bed early. And in the great night of São Geraldo at last some thing was happening whose confused and dusty meaning they vainly were trying by day to sing with open mouths. Listening in their sleep, squirming, summoned and unable to go, disturbed by the irreplaceable importance that each thing and each being has in a city being born. But Cristina would goad them at the next meeting. Her presence was enough to agitate the group and, soon enough, amid projects of purity and love for the soul, without a brighter word able to be uttered in the gloomy meeting room, they'd all be excited toward the path of goodness: Cristina is our vanguard, they'd say smiling. It was a sneaky attempt at wit where it was least expected. While Cristina with an ease of intelligence was establishing new principles: the life that you carry within is not worldly, she'd say, the sacrifice of the flesh is to be fulfilled as flesh, she'd say. The factories would whistle announcing the end of work. Soon you'd also hear the stores' iron gratings coming down—but the girls were having trouble separating from each other and in the already dark room were moving about not knowing what to do.

Cristina was a young woman short as a woman should be, a little fat as a woman ought to be. She was the most advanced girl in the township. Which didn't mean she attracted the attention of men. These, more innocent and loyal than the women of São Geraldo, would approach her out of a certain curiosity: she smelled of milk, sweat, clothes of the body— they'd just sniff and walk away.

When Lucrécia joined the A.F.Y.S.G. she already found the members allowing themselves so much spiritual liberty that they no longer knew what to be. From exteriorizing themselves so much they'd ended up like the flowers they sang of, gaining a meaning that went beyond the existence of each one, getting worked up like the already restless streets of São Geraldo. They'd finally formed the type of person adapted to living at that time in a township.

Lucrécia had approached attracted by the idea of dances but Cristina and she looked at each other from the first moment as enemies; except Lucrécia wasn't intelligent and was defeated. Moreover everything there seemed strange to the girl, and the word "ideal," which the others used so much, sounded unfamiliar to her. "The ideal, the ideal!" but what did they mean by the ideal! she said to them stubborn and even haughty. The girls, confused, exchanged glances spitefully. Lucrécia didn't take long to retreat while Cristina was gaining in strength, becoming crueler and happier. And soon the disturbance caused by Lucrécia was forgotten. Just as the population had already stopped blaming the horses.

The horses, now unnoticed out of habit, were nonetheless the cunning power over São Geraldo. And Lucrécia too, ignored by the Association.

The girl and a horse represented the two races of builders that had initiated the tradition of the future metropolis, both could figure on its coat of arms. The measly function of the girl in her time was an archaic function that is reborn every time a town is formed, her history formed with effort the spirit of a city. You couldn't know which kingdom she'd represent at the new colony since her work was all too brief, and almost unexploitable: everything that she was seeing was *some thing*. In her and in a horse the impression was the expression. Really a very crude function—she would indicate the intimate names of things, she, the horses and a few others; and later things would be looked at by that name. Reality was needing the girl in order to have a shape. "What is seen"—was her only inner life; and what was seen became her vague history. Which if revealed to her would only give her the recollection of a thought that crossed her mind before falling asleep. Despite not being able to recognize herself in the revelation of her secret life, she really was directing it; she was aware of it indirectly as the plant would be touched if its root were wounded. It was in her small irreplaceable destiny to pass through the greatness of spirit as if through a danger, and then decline in the wealth of

an age of gold and darkness, and then disappear from view—
that's what happened to São Geraldo.

The idea of "progressing," the Association's, had found Lucrécia with already awakened attention, wanting to get out
of the difficulty and even use it—because difficulty was her
only tool. Until reaching the extreme docility of vision. Wagons were going by. The church was ringing its bells. Enslaved
horses were trotting. The tower of the power plant in the sun.
All this could be seen from a window, sniffing the new air. And
the city started taking the shape that her gaze was revealing.

At this opportune moment in which people were living, each
time something was seen—new extensions would emerge, and
one more meaning would be created: that was the hardly us-
able intimate life of Lucrécia Neves. And this was São Geraldo, whose future History, as in the memory of a buried city,
would be just the history of what had been seen.

Even Spiritist centers were starting to form diffidently in
the Catholic township and Lucrécia herself made up that she'd
sometimes hear a voice. But in fact it would be easier for her
to see the supernatural: touching reality is what would make
her fingers tremble. She'd never heard a voice, or even wished
to hear one; she was less important, and much busier.

And that's how São Geraldo was heaped up with creaky
wagons, houses and markets, with plans for building a bridge.
You could hardly make out its radiant and peaceful moistness that on certain mornings would come from the mist and
emerge from the nostrils of the horses—the radiant moistness was one of the most difficult realities to distinguish in
the township. From the highest window of the Convent, on
a Sunday—after crossing downtown, the Gate and the train
depot—people would lean out and discern the moistness

through the dusk: there … there was the township extended. And what they were seeing was the thought that they could never think. "It's the loveliest promenade in São Geraldo," they'd then say nodding. And there was no other way to get to know the township; São Geraldo was exploitable only with the gaze. Lucrécia Neves too standing was watching the city that from within was invisible and that distance was turning into a dream once again: she'd lean out without any individuality, trying only to look directly at things.

The Sunday pilgrimage to the Convent now over, the houses lighting up one by one—the more you penetrated the center of a city the less you'd know what a city is like.

Ah, if I could go this very day to a dance, the girl was thinking on that Sunday night, gently touching the little table in the living room. She really liked having fun. Content, standing beside the little table, laughing at the idea of a dance, her yellow teeth innocently showing.

But at least she'd take walks as much as she could, among the things in the Market, in her hat, with her purse, the odd run in her stockings. She'd come in and out of the house, or keep busy for hours with clothes, transforming, mending; she had a few boyfriends and got tired a lot; with her hat and old gloves she'd cross the Fish Market.

And she'd take walks. Even with Doctor Lucas, when they'd bump into each other, their relationship almost that of patient and doctor, his wife ill in the São Geraldo Sanatorium, and Lucrécia Neves proud to walk around with a man with a degree—they'd go down six cement steps toward the park that stretched out beneath the township's level. Moist leaves were lying on the ground—they'd walk looking at the ground. And from the plants a new smell was coming, of some thing that was being built and that only the future would see.

The park of São Geraldo was yellow and gray with long blackened stalks—and butterflies. And that was her friendship with a young and austere man. If Lucrécia Neves wasn't sensual the difference between the sexes gave her a certain happiness. In the park was some playground equipment, black lampposts, soldiers with their girlfriends—it was one of the promenades of São Geraldo. Doctor Lucas had lent her a book once but she had a hard time taking it in, as if out of stubbornness and excessive patience. Anyway she'd never needed intelligence. They sat on a slope and because he wrote for the "Socio-Medical Journal" the girl said maybe one day he'd write the story of his life! she said and looked up to the sky with haughtiness. Everything was a lie and it was getting cold, the doctor was advising her—and she deep down possessing that happy unease that was mistrust about whatever might come from a man: the girl was very mistrustful. And slow. For she'd talk and talk with the doctor and couldn't convey anything to him. But at least she was peering at everything with such clarity: she was seeing soldiers and children. Her form of expression boiled down to taking a good look, she so enjoyed going on walks!—and that's how the inhabitants of São Geraldo were, perhaps inspired by the sharpness of the air throughout that region, prone to heavy rains and to high summers. Even when she was little Lucrécia would already keep her eyes open for hours in bed, listening to the noise of the odd wagon that passing by would seem to mark her earthly destiny. While in other places happier children, daughters of fishermen, were going out to sea. Later, having grown, the children in the early morning were no longer home—they'd return dirty, ragged, with some thing in their hands.

Perhaps summoned by the beginning of the vision she'd had from the window of the Convent, on Monday the girl was seeking São Geraldo's other promenade: the stream. She'd pass through the Gate and cross the rails, quickly descend the slope while peering at her feet. For an instant immobilized she'd seem to reflect deeply. Though she wasn't thinking about anything. And suddenly, irrepressible, she'd go in the opposite direction—climb the hill in the pasture, tired from her own persistence. As she'd climb she'd make out on the left a ruined section of the township, the blackened houses … Up ahead you couldn't see anything but the same ascending line that would finally settle on the hill.

Where she'd stand peering out. Still breathless from the climb. Serious, obedient. Finding only the clouds that were passing and the great brightness. But she didn't seem disappointed.

Despite the clear sky the air on the hill was blustery and, at times unrestrained, would violently drag a piece of paper or a leaf. The tin cans and the flies couldn't quite populate the field. At this time of day you'd trample ardent weeds and couldn't subjugate with a glance the dryness and the wind of the plateau—a wave of dust rising with the gallop of an imaginary horse. The girl was waiting patiently. What sort of resemblance had she come seeking on the hill? she was peering out. Until the end of the afternoon started awakening the blinking moisture that the afternoon makes rise in the countryside. And the possibility of murmuring that darkness favors.

But at night horses relieved of their burdens and put out to pasture would gallop slender and free in the dark. Foals, ponies, sorrels, long mares, hard hooves—a horse's cold and dark head—hooves beating, muzzles foaming rising toward the air in rage and grumbling. And sometimes a sigh that would chill the grasses with tremors. Then the bay would go ahead. He was sidling past, his head leaning down to his chest, galloping smoothly. The others were watching without looking.

Sitting halfway up in bed Lucrécia Neves would sense the dry hooves advancing until halting on the highest point of the hill. And the head dominating the township, letting out its long neigh. Fear would overtake her in the darkness of the room, the terror of a king, the young girl would want to respond displaying her gums. In the envy of desire her face would take on the restless nobility of a horse's head. Tired, jubilant, listening to the sleepwalking trot. She'd hardly left her room when her form would start swelling and firming up, and when she'd reach the street she'd already be galloping with sensitive feet, her hooves sliding down the final steps. From the deserted sidewalk she'd look at: one corner and another. And she'd see things as a horse sees them. Because there was no time to lose: even at night the city was at work fortifying itself and in the morning new trenches would be ready. From her bed she'd at least try to listen to the hill in the pasture where in the dark nameless horses were galloping returned to the state of hunting and war. Until she'd fall asleep.

But the beasts didn't abandon the township. And if amidst the wild patrol a white colt appeared—it was a fright in the dark. All of them would halt. The prodigious horse *would appear*. It would display itself rearing for an instant. Motionless the animals would wait without glancing at each other. But one of them would stomp its hoof. And the brief thump would break the night watch: spurred on they'd suddenly advance lively, crisscrossing without touching and among them the white horse would be lost. Until a neigh of sudden anger would warn them—for a second watchful, they'd soon spread out in a new composition of trotting, their backs without riders, their necks lowered until their mouths touched their chests. Their manes bristling; rhythmic, uncultured.

The late night would find them motionless in the dark. Stable and weightless. There they were, invisible, breathing. Waiting with brief intelligence. Below, in the sleeping township, a rooster was flying and perching on the ledge of a window. The hens were watching. Beyond the railroad a rat ready to flee.

Then the dapple-gray stomped its foot. Nobody had a mouth to speak with but one would give a small signal that would sound off from space to space in the darkness. They were peering out. Those animals that had one eye for seeing on each side—nothing was seen straight on, and that was the night of São Geraldo, the flanks of a horse quivering in a quick contraction. In the first silences a mare would open wide her eyes as if surrounded by eternity. The most restless colt was still raising its mane in a deaf neigh. Finally silence would reign.

Until dawn would reveal them. They were spread out, standing on the hill. Exhausted, cool.

And on the threshold of morning, when all were sleeping and the light had hardly separated from the moisture of the trees—on the threshold of morning the highest point of the city would become Efigênia.

From the slightly more livid horizon a bird was rising, and over by the railroad the mists were passing. The well-spaced trees still kept the motionlessness of the night. Only the blades of grass were trembling in the fresh breeze, in the meadow a sheet of old paper was vibrating. Efigênia was getting up and looking at the plain whose former roughness had been smoothed by the wind of so many nights. She'd touch the light of the windowpane wiping it with her elbow. Then she'd kneel and pray the only sentence that had stayed with her from the Sisters orphanage, from that time when the highest window of the Convent opened onto a lost village: I feel in my flesh a law that contradicts the law of my spirit, she was saying absently. What her flesh was, she'd never found out; in this moment it was a kneeling form. What her spirit was, she didn't know. Maybe it was the hardly risen morning light above the tracks. Her body had only served her as a sign in order to be seen; her spirit, she was seeing it on the plain. Scratching herself violently in her transfiguration: you could no longer say she was small because when kneeling she'd lose her recognizable form. Rheumatism was her hardship. And such did she muster herself diffuse on the brightness of her spirit above the meadow that her spirit was already no longer hers. She would stay like this, thinking through the intermediary of the light she was seeing. The sheet of paper went flying across the plain, had nestled against a tree and was trembling trapped against the trunk. I feel in my flesh a law that contradicts the law of my spirit, she was saying clearing her throat in the dawn: everything was quivering more and more though nothing was transformed.

But behold a sheet of paper vibrating in steel amidst the dark foliage like a sign in order to be seen. Efigênia was getting up with effort, recuperating her dry form and entering the kitchen. The pans were cold, and the stove dead. Soon the flame was rising, smoke filling the compartment and the woman coughing with eyes full of tears. Wiping them, opening the back door and spitting.

The earth of the yard was hard. In the space the clothesline.

Efigênia was rubbing her hands warming them: all that was about to be transformed by her gaze. A gaze that didn't come from her eyes but from her stone face—that's how others saw her and knew there was no point in complaining. Looking at that face they were supposed to hide their weakness, show their crudeness and not expect praise—that was how Efigênia was good and merciless. She'd head back to the kitchen, swallow a few gulps of coffee while blowing on it, coughing, spitting, filling herself with the first heat. Then she'd open the door and the smoke was freed. Standing in the doorway, without imploring, without mercy.

Behold the neutral brightness covering the meadow. Dark birds were flying. All the foliage was now pierced by light, gravity and fragrance. The woman was spitting into the distance with more confidence, hands on her hips. Her jewel-like hardness. The clothesline was swaying under the weight of a sparrow. She was spitting again, gruff, happy. Her spirit's work had been done: it was day.

2   The Citizen

"MARINE BEINGS, WHEN NOT AFFIXED TO THE SEA floor, adapt to a drifting or pelagic life," Perseu studied on the afternoon of May 15, 192...

Heroic and empty the citizen remained standing beside the open window. But in fact he could never transmit to anyone the way in which he was harmonious, and even if he spoke he wouldn't say a word that conveyed the graciousness of his appearance: his extreme harmony was simply evident.

"Pelagic animals reproduce with profusion," he said with hollow luminosity. Blind and glorious—that was all that could be known of him seeing him from the street at a third-story window. But if no one could ever fathom his harmony—neither did he seem to feel any more than that. Because this was his degree of light. "Marine animals and plants with profusion," he said without a push but without brakes because this was his degree of light. It didn't matter that in the light he was as blind as others in the dark. The difference is that he was in the light. "Drifting," he said. Unnoticed at the window because he was simply one of the modes of being São Geraldo. And also one of its founders only for having been born when the township too was being erected, just for having a last name that would only become strange when one day São Geraldo changed its name; standing in front of the open window. That was the nature of a race of man.

And that's how he remained, observing with dedication Efigênia who in the street was carrying a basket. The woman stopped and while resting let her eye wander idly and with a certain despair over the sunny surroundings: it was almost three and all the doors started opening at the same time. Efigênia picked the basket back up. Only to stop again a bit farther on and ruefully drag her load. Finally she halted once more— but Perseu was patient. "The animals," he said. The woman picked the basket back up. "Reproduce with extraordinary profusion," Perseu said. To memorize was beautiful. While you were memorizing you didn't think, the vast thought was the body existing—his concretization was luminous: he was motionless in front of a window. "They feed on basic microvegetation, infusoria, etc."

"Etc.!" he repeated shining, unconquerable.

And now he was quieting down, sluggish and full of sun. "Marine beings," he said in a murmur; the boy's unawareness was broadly dominating the city. "Reproduce," he added somberly. His wings were great motionless wings. He then leaned out the window and shouted:

"Fruit seller! come up!"

Ah! flew a frightened crow.

Big, revealed in his naked arms, he bought tangerines in the dark hallway.

He returned and perched on the windowsill. Soon he was eating and tossing the seeds into the dirty alley. Looking while blinking: the seed would bounce twice before becoming motionless in the sun. Perseu didn't lose sight of it despite the distance and the people who were already crossing back and forth hurriedly: he was patient. And soon the street was ending up full of concrete points: countless seeds spread out in an arrangement that had a blatant meaning—except it was incomprehensible. Like the houses arranged along the street. It was in his nature to be able to possess an idea and not know how to think it: obfuscated, persistent, tossing seeds, that's how he'd explain it. There were even a few anecdotes about the slow intelligence of the men of São Geraldo, whereas the women were so clever! "They reproduce with extraordinary profusion!" said the young man suddenly spurred on.

Before long he was once again absorbed by the kind of perfection that existed in tossing seeds; everything that resembled mechanisms was already starting to interest the new citizens. He, absorbed yet remote. Since his time seemed impossible to be filled by an action: he was tossing seeds into the void. It was just that some sign was making it so that inside that breadth was his life specifically. "Pelagic marine beings," he said quite loudly with his mouth full.

What was saving this lost creature from anguish is that he was lost as God wanted one to be innocent: he ate and tossed the seeds. The world could do without this blind bricklayer. But since he was living, no one else could carry out his work, so intransmissible it had already become: so he tossed three more seeds, drawing back his head and aiming with one eye shut ... "A life drifting or pelagic," he exclaimed pulling himself together. Behind his beautiful and resigned face was another that, repeating his external features, had a somewhat horrible expression, the expression of a deep thought. And a moral intolerance—the intolerance of São Geraldo's people—both larger and more amorphous than that of the exterior face that was seeking a certain unity that could be immediately understood by a mirror:

behind the golden and courteous face an almost disagreeable whiff of the stable because he was still quite young.

Thus several proportional and ripened moments had passed while the young man was tossing the seeds as if he'd been refining gold in a workshop—the first ringing of the bells made him lift a face made sleepy by its concentration. For an instant a countenance beyond reach was waiting without interest for whatever they were going to say to him: the clock in the square was striking three broad hours over São Geraldo and beneath the vibrant ringing the township was sinking. When it reappeared dripping with the last echoes, the township was bright and everything could be more seen: on the table by the window the open book was resting, and on the page revealed by the sudden clarity of the hour was inscribed:

"This discoidal animal is formed according to the symmetry based on the number 4."

That's what it said! And the sun was beating down on the dusty page: a cockroach was even climbing the house across the street ... Then the young man said something as lustrous as a scarab:

"Pelagic animals reproduce with extraordinary profusion," he finally exclaimed from memory.

The delayed church clock struck three. Ah! the crow pursued again was terrified. Perseu shook the last two seeds in the palm of his hand and threw them as dice. Game over! It was afternoon. The young man stopped astonished and empty. Unexpectedly he opened his great wings in a yawn of youth.

3   *The Hunt*

ON THAT SAME AFTERNOON THE CADENCE OF HOOVES was heard on the stones of Market Street. The wagon and the horse were picking up the pace. Suddenly the horse's head grew, with one frightened movement of the neck it arose: purple gums appeared and the bridles cut into its mouth—in a neighing of its whole body and in the stridency of the wheels: the horse and the wagon. Then the wind kept blowing in silence.

What was happening on the street had no effect but was calling out as if to watch a fire.

In her bedroom a young woman was standing and, if trying to keep her wits about her, was already finding herself surrendered to sound itself without language. Also in the room the objects, in a constant way, had become unbearable beyond a few seconds—the girl always had her back turned to some thing; the room had already rushed ahead, heavy with ornaments. She alone was still too aware to go ahead with the disguise, the wind between the houses was rushing her.

While she was taking off her shoes she was even goading on the confusion of the room and the street, from which she'd take her own shape. Nothing however had yet pushed her toward the reality of what was happening. In the gloomy chamber the brightness was the keyhole.

Finally the choice of a hat made her concentrate letting her catch up with the room. She opened the drawer and from the darkness into the air brought her most ornate hat. She sought with care a new way to wear it. Her urge was hard and would never burst into tears: with the hat pushed down to her forehead she looked at herself in the mirror. She was making herself inexpressive and with empty eyes as if this were the most real way to see herself. She couldn't quite reach herself however, charmed by the deep unreality of her image. She ran her fingers over her tongue, moistened her brows … then looked at herself with severity.

The scarlet roses on the wall were unattainable in the mirror, bunches of roses that from being so motionless moved forward.

Until touched by her own attention, she started to see herself with difficulty.

Lucrécia Neves would never be beautiful. She had however a surplus of beauty that doesn't exist in pretty people. The hair upon which the fantastic hat rested was ample; and the many black spots spread out in the light of her skin gave her an external tone to be touched by fingers. Only her straight eyebrows ennobled her face, where something vulgar existed like a barely sensitive sign of the future of her narrow and deep soul. Her whole nature didn't seem to reveal itself: it was a habit of hers to lean forward when talking to people, her eyes half-closed— she'd seem then, like the township itself, excited by an event that wasn't set in motion. Her face was inexpressive unless a thought made it hesitate.

Though it wasn't this possibility of wit and sweetness that

she was making the most of. It was whatever rigidity there was in a face that the girl, getting ready, would accentuate. And once she was ready—disguising herself with a superficiality that didn't try to draw attention to the body but to its adornments—her figure would hide itself beneath emblems and symbols, and in her intense charm the girl would resemble an ideal portrait of herself. Which didn't please her—it was work.

She suddenly leaned toward the mirror and sought the loveliest way to see herself, opened her mouth, looked at her teeth, closed it … Soon, from her fixed gaze, was emerging at last the way of not penetrating too much and of looking with slight effort only at the surface—and of quickly no longer looking. The girl looked: her ears were white among her tangled strands of hair from which was emerging a face that the sprinkled spots were making tremble—and without lingering, because she'd overreach by going too far: this was the loveliest way to see herself!

She sighed impatient, courageous. She closed and opened her eyes, opened her mouth excessively in order to peer at her teeth: and for a rare instant saw herself with a red tongue, in an apparition of beauty and calm horror … She breathed more satisfied, without knowing why rejoicing: in the closed room, full of delicate chairs, everything was getting so burlesque with a red tongue! the young lady laughed with gravity as if she had a dwarf to torment. She then continued the disguise. Pleased, silent and crude while climbing into her patent leather shoes. Now she really was taller and more daring, the clarion gave the call to plunder.

But in fact her superficiality was a severe stripping-down and when she was ready she'd look like an object, an object of São Geraldo. That's what she was working on ferociously with calm.

While she was dressing the intimate murmuring with which she was dressing was slowly transforming itself into a terribly mischievous stupidity: she was looking at the roses on the wallpaper playing dumb inside, somehow imitating the existence of the wardrobe she was rifling through in search of the bracelet. She was touching one thing or another as if reality were whatever was unreachable. And it was—with a little tap on the dust of her shoe—Lucrécia Neves saw that it was, though she laughed foolishly, the horse neighing in the street down below—with a little tap on the dust of her shoe she was seeing the various shapes of the room, the roses, the chair! but she was ignoring a certain stubbornness that the fact of having imitated the wardrobe had brought her—and kept looking for the bracelet.

What is it you're looking for, my flower? she was wondering without interrupting herself. She also saw the bed with hard vivacity—which immediately transformed into a more vehement search for the bracelet. Tired. Since she alone had worked: how to stop seeing that the things in the room hadn't transformed themselves for as much as an instant? there they were. Just a moment of weakness, and once again whatever she had built through so many glances would be destroyed … And Lucrécia Neves saw with surprise an unconquerable, silent room—with great surprise at not finding the bracelet.

Once again working furiously, throwing shoes to one side and handkerchiefs to the other, searching. As she was opening and closing drawers, from the drawers opened and closed and half-closed and opened, planes and rectangles were already being reborn, edges being rebuilt, more exposed surfaces aging, heights straightening themselves out: in appalled retreats her glances had recreated the reality of the room. A bit mistrustful, innocent amidst the wreckage … And the bracelet? she was scratching herself, now without majesty, looking around covered in dust, charmed, almost near-sighted—she who had such clear eyes. She was searching for the bracelet by squatting to look under the bed, whining wounded with an animal's delicateness: "where is it, my God," she kept saying scratching herself.

Finally removing from the drawer like real pearls her fake jewels, lifting them to her face, giving glory and hope to the room. Where she stopped almost ready. Looking around stupidly, with the difficulty of thought that her lack of sensuality would bring her. What was missing was the perfume!

Just like that she embalmed herself with perfume, shaking herself all over.

But it was day, would the sunlight full of wind that was blowing beyond the balcony annul all her adornments? Because she'd dressed trying to recreate the strength of former festive nights, imagining she'd encounter on dirty Market Street the elite of a ball, prestige and extraordinary manners—where girls would laugh having trouble behaving; and where she'd say out loud, threatening with her finger: you're bad, Joaquim!

Yes! yes! a ball would be the city of stone surrendering at last: or a military band, a circus! the carousel! or to approach stiff all over the family house transformed into a ball.

A ball in São Geraldo: the night stultified by the rain and she treading with her hooves on the slippery stone, and the groups of umbrellas arriving. Groups of anonymous gentlemen, the wooden gentlemen around whom people were dancing. She was closing the soaking wet umbrella. And when the brass band burst out everyone would join in. The first steps were taken far from the body, blindly testing the ground. But soon thereafter the dramatic music would draw them in. The trombone was resounding isolated above the melody. Through the windows, in the tepid ballroom, the girl was quickly seeing in the little English waltz the rivulets of rain turning gold awakened beneath the lamps of the courtyard, raising sleepy smoke: it was raining on the deserted courtyard, and she was dancing. With painted cheeks and resistant eyes, expressing; what could she be celebrating? she was dancing in a new composition of trotting. And outside it was raining in silence. Lucrécia Neves was returning from the ball with dusty feet; the nausea of the waltz and of the intimate men was whirling still in her organs because some very similar thing had happened to São Geraldo: she'd danced, it was raining, the drops running beneath the light, she dancing, and the city erected all around.

The memory of the dance was ravishing her in the bedroom where, decked out like an engraving of a saint, she was ready to go out. With her face immobilized by the disguise the girl examined herself in the mirror.

She was golden and crude in the shadow.

That's how she'd created herself. Though she still needed to create voluptuousness in that face to which selfishness gave a loyal character: she then tinted her lips by moistening with saliva the crimson paper.

With her mouth dirty her face became childlike, smaller and guilty. In the mirror her elegance had the fallible quality of overly lovely things without root ... in a quick emotion she slammed the door of the room, cried with a voice suddenly tragic and broken: mama I'm going out! went down the stairs again slowly, making sure not to slip in the shadows with her horseshoes.

That's how she was going out into the street, looking both

ways. She really would have liked to give up at last and rest. Sometimes she'd even imagine, smiling in ecstasy, boarding a ship and heading to sea forever. But her journey was by land.

The wind greeted her on the street, the girl halted protecting her eyes wounded by the light. And suddenly the brightness revealed her.

The possibilities had ceased: she was dressed in blue, full of ribbons and bracelets. Her red hat was pushed down to her eyebrows by the power of the insurmountable taste of fashion. Her scarlet purse had beads ... But she found such a blank street! Without the errors or the mending with which she'd built herself in her room ... Even the sparrow on the branch was chirping without possible error because it was the first time ... and was this a street in the afternoon?

Once again she'd badly imitated São Geraldo. Which at this hour was almost chaste ... The open afternoon was revealing as much as possible the beads and necklaces. She'd brought useless weapons.

Soon however she was leaving the bottom of the staircase with a dry sigh, straightening up without wriggling in order not to collapse, moving forward with a certain insolence. The same insolence that would make her buy hats that rarely imitated nature: without birds, without flowers, her hats seemed to be made of hats, with variations in the brims themselves — and which she'd wear the way she'd grasp an object.

Gradually Lucrécia Neves had pulled herself back together after the collision with the light and once again seemed taller and like a pursuer. She was walking with a daintiness of expression, without joy. Her balance upon the heels of her ankle-high boots was so difficult that she was walking between balance and imbalance, kept in the air by her little open parasol.

It wasn't without constant effort that she was maintaining her elegance right then because she'd dressed in the potent darkness of a bedroom, perhaps in order to be seen at night. And the day in São Geraldo wasn't the future, it was hard, finished streets. The girl was feeling inferior to that merciless clarity. So current! so current, she was seeing thrown into whatever was happening. She was looking around greedily, so current! she was doing everything possible not to go beyond it, adjusting the bracelets that were colliding on her wrists.

The clock struck four. For a moment it seemed to wait for an answer. Perseu Maria saw that he was late and started walking faster. His feeling was one of calm and joy because his body was big while marching—steps were climbed, cobblestones stepped on. He was big while marching. And he didn't know what he was thinking because he was strong. At a certain point he said, in the exterior intimacy with which he was seeing himself walking, he said in a grievous hesitation that came from a certain awareness of his solitude: "the ground." That's what he thought as a child says: "the ground." But when he raised his eyes from his deep dream he realized he wasn't late. Lucrécia right then was approaching the place where they'd agreed to meet. The fellow stopped on the corner blocked by the truck. The girl stopped on the other corner waiting. They looked at each other. He looked at her. What a face!

He was thinking.

Finally he thought more clearly: "the face." When he'd see her from far off he'd see her better. With bracelets and beads she was looking like a victim. Perseu added the thought with dazzled difficulty: "what a face she's got," he saw with still greater clarity.

"Salutations …," said the girl.

"Salutations," he replied embarrassed by the joke.

And so it was that, just because of Lucrécia's presence, he turned entirely dark in the shadow, morose, losing the least bit of singularity. The girl too was breathing modest, calm. On the threshold of São Geraldo they were roughly stripping themselves down as much as possible. They became so simple that they became unattainable. And they started strolling through the city.

Old roaches were coming out of the sewers. From the basements the cellars were suffocating the streets with the smell of rotten rinds. But the saws in the workshops were buzzing in bees and gold throughout the township, almost empty at this hour of extreme brightness.

From a higher railing the young man and the girl saw an old woman with an open parasol at the other railing—the township rising and falling in prison staircases.

Market Street still smelled of the fish sold in the morning, in the rivulets running to the sewer were floating scales and the odd soft clove. With the experience of childhood the two were easily steering clear of the straw baskets, passing alertly through the smell of the Iron Crown Charcoal Works, and strolling down narrower streets. The salamis hanging in the doorway of the store were smelling like the back of a house. They smelled it. Finally reaching the Gate.

They checked by leaning forward that no train was coming. The wind over the tracks blew in their faces. They crossed.

Past the railway the neighborhood buildings were becoming more spread-out; already you could see really just a few houses. And soon they were strolling beneath telegraph wires. The air was pure and blank as in a salt flat—the girl was looking at the sky taking care to make sure her hat didn't move, the sky—"what a sight," she was thinking indecipherably. She was staring at the serene afternoon on the stones, on the rusty tools on the ground—the dry trash was flying around … Everything was real but as if seen through a mirror. For a moment the girl was seeking a way to be and didn't know; excessively calm, untouchable.

But when they reached the top of the hill in the pasture Perseu pointed out the city with his finger.

The poise of his finger over the void, the wind, the wind … —his mourning hat flew, he ran after it when suddenly the township made itself known at last because a hat had flown in the wind! the young man went past the barbed wire running with open arms, his delicate mouth biting the air. Lucrécia followed him with her eyes until he vanished from sight … She then set to waiting, without comprehension, without incomprehension.

Soon she was veering off a bit, dreaming of walking alone with a dog and being seen on the hill: like the postcard of a city. Lucrécia Neves needed countless things: a checkered skirt and a little hat of the same material; for a long time now she'd been needing to feel how others would see her in a checkered skirt and hat, a belt right on her hips and a flower in the belt: dressed like that she'd look at the township and it would be transformed. With a dog. That's how you composed a vision. The girl didn't have any imagination but a watchful reality of things that was making her almost sleepwalk; she was needing things in order for them to exist.

Perseu brought the hat back and wiping it on his sleeve looked at her laughing with worry, unable to prevent the victory of having caught it; laughing and looking with disquiet at the calm nature of the world. He then thought with wisdom of what he could say to her: "looks like it's gonna rain, huh, Lucrécia!", just so they could be in agreement again and in order to make turn toward him the face of the girl which was looking insistently at the tower below. But it was a lie: the bright sky was enveloping them and losing them. When he placed the hat on his head the fellow had forgotten what it was he'd been pointing at.

He still tried with one finger but withdrew it quickly. Nearby lay the mountain of trash waiting to be burned … And the conversation had wrapped up. Lucrécia Neves, looking, wasn't smiling.

Only the air was still open, black wires connecting the poles from bottom to top — "what a sight," Lucrécia was seeing while looking from bottom to top. The little birds were flying imitating each other without tiring. Radio wires were crossing clean and slender the air breathable with cold in the fields … they were looking from bottom to top. Motionless. If it were possible for someone to understand and not draw any conclusions — that's the way the young man was looking deeply. And the way the girl didn't understand had the same clarity that understandable things had, the same perfection to which both belonged: black wires were swinging in the colorlessness — they were looking from bottom to top, motionless, incomprehensible, constant. What a sight! Lucrécia Neves finally thought.

Then Perseu moved his head toward the air and gazed at the railroad below.

Everything was stirred by the young man's stupid and gentle gaze, everything was hesitating in the wind, and existing within itself, without smell, without taste, with the irreplaceable form of the track itself, of the piled-up wood itself—and of the green, green countryside. "Just look! the dry trough for the horses." The two of them were so slow and difficult that they were seeing with obstinacy the thing of which things were made, and which was enveloping the girl's face with the same stridency of the beetle atop that stem. "Just look at the beetle!" They looked at the beetle. Lucrécia and Perseu were watching with wrinkled noses. Perseu was going from himself to the girl and from her to himself without noticing, his eyelids blinking from the sun and from a stubborn thought of love, which he didn't know how to give her. "And there really was no reason to give her love"—he grabbed a stone and wiped it clean of dust showing an intimacy with dirty things that Lucrécia Neves looked at attentively without understanding— "there really was no reason." Only reasons not to; and one of them is that "she was really picky," the young man accused her and maybe only his mother, who'd been dead for a year now, would have understood that this could be a man's accusation. Lucrécia Neves's lack of fatigue was also making him wary. She was like one of those foreigners who'd say: "that's how it is in my country." Perseu's narrow forehead was seeking something on which to take amorous pity but even his girlfriend's physical defects were calm, her accepting them just by saying: that's how it is in my country! seeming protected by a race of people just like her. Even her pleasures were made of the idea that a night spent in a tent would be so nice, that getting up in the morning was no effort, that a soldier's life wasn't hard— she'd always humiliated him with her love for men in uniform, showing great admiration for their physical courage and for their weapons, of which he was ashamed—so tactless! he'd think, and feel that there was something there of which she could be accused.

Which didn't keep the two of them just then from being placed on equal footing by the same instant of youth on the hill in the pasture—walking and talking on their way back, their hands moving in explanatory gestures. It didn't matter what they were saying to each other so excitedly: they themselves were meant to be seen, like the city. And if someone had seen them from afar he'd make out an acrobat and a king. Walking quickly was making them happy—the king was smiling and was handsome, the acrobat was exerting herself with funny faces: there was a lack of mechanical control in the way both of them walked—they were a single person with one short leg and one long one, the beauty of the young man and the horror, the flower and the insect, one short leg and one long one climbing up, down, up. Sometimes the young man would seem to pull ahead and the girl was dancing around him: that's when he'd smile divine and pure, and Lucrécia Neves would speak— and that's how others would see them.

Or on the other hand she was the one who'd stopped up ahead in the wind.

Had they quarreled? He hesitant while looking at her. When she'd seem to him destructible like that, the fellow out of compassion and disappointment would become rude. He even felt like saying to her: ah, I'm not what you think, honey, you won't do whatever you like to me!—though he knew, as he was looking at the stones, that she wouldn't do anything to him and neither would he to her—because that's how they were and up ahead was the stream.

"What do you think I did yesterday?" said Perseu Maria presumptuous.

In vain he was trying, seeing her at times ugly and looking at the dark spots on her skin, to protect with a man's love the feebleness of her figure: the thin mouth that wasn't laughing, on each cheek those circles of rouge that scandalized the neighbors …"she sure did like to show off."

Even the girl's dreams: he himself had never dreamed of statues, he thought with extreme reluctance. He seemed to think that dreaming of statues was going too far. Moving the stone between his fingers, Perseu looked at Lucrécia quickly: he didn't know how to admire her. He contorted his narrow forehead. When he'd think, his face would get even more prominent and indecisive—he who would get so happy when, taking the train, he'd go to the beach, the exercises and the laughter, and under the sun his youthful body … Which girls in swimsuits would look at surrendering, feeling him to be strong and innocent—he was one of the new men of São Geraldo.

"Papa's complaining about the house," he said throwing the stone attentively far away. "It's full of flies … Last night I felt mosquitoes, moths, flying cockroaches, who knows what else landing on us."

"It is I," said Lucrécia Neves with great irony.

Perseu looked at the ground, ashamed, sorrowful and calm. Keenly trying to disrupt such immodesty through his own interest in the weeds on the ground … Because the girl had tossed into the air her bright face where her spots were getting blacker and blacker, things that darken in the winter light. Her brashness was horrible, sometimes she had no shame. He enduring her little games with agony, looking at her quickly and diverting his eyes. But twisting her lips in still greater sarcasm, she said:

"Hold on to your hat or it'll fly off again, just think!"

She thought it was ridiculous for a man to wear a hat …, he was well aware. Ah, she doesn't understand me, the fellow thought, pushed with both hands the hat onto his head, looking at her radiant: the vague cold had given the girl goose bumps … but she was cheerful! How impossible to embrace her, he reflected worried, because she'd always make some movement that would make both of them too big, he ashamed to be a man and feeling like laughing …

"… what's up … don't you recognize me!"

But he laughed happy into the air …

And suddenly time raced by with the breeze over the countryside, they walked and were already at the Gate.

They made sure no train was coming, the wind from the rails hit them in the face—they crossed quickly.

Time was racing by and it seemed to Lucrécia that the house across the way was undoubtedly tall, the pavement smooth, the stone dark, it seemed to her that the sewer was shining—and the girl no longer knew how to see! For an instant she broke her caution and looked immodestly at the stone, the house, this world. Even without holding herself back, she could see only the narrow street, the stone pavement, windows … She wanted at least to push into that same instant the dress and the hat, and compose São Geraldo, but she put it off for Felipe, and both were walking excited, silent and fatigued. Perseu had taken off his hat because of the sun and was clasping it to his chest. From a certain distance they looked like street musicians who'd come from very far away—and whatever other people could see was making Lucrécia Neves walk full of pride, showing herself off; the young man's lips were opening dry and laughing. How happy they were! the breeze was blowing over the township.

Lucrécia Neves might have wanted to express it, imitating with thought the wind that knocks on doors—but she was missing the name of things. She was missing the name of things, but behold, look here, there, behold the thing, the church, the doves flying over the Library, the salamis in the doorway of the store, the burning glass of a window signaling insistently to the hill ...

The two of them standing watching. And the hardness of things was the girl's most clipped way of seeing. From the impossibility of overcoming that resistance was emerging, in green fruit, the tang of firm things over which was blowing with heroism that civic wind that makes flags flutter! the city was an unconquerable fortress! And she trying at least to imitate what she was seeing: things were practically right there! and there! But you had to repeat them. The girl was trying to repeat with her eyes whatever she was seeing, that would yet be the only way of taking possession. Her voice couldn't take it and was fraying, her hair sticking out from under her stiff hat—and entering Market Street, the wind lifting her skirt, she clasping her hat with both hands—everything that was resting as trash in the dry gutters was awakened by the wind; despite the firmness, how reversible the township was just from the wind! a little dark bird flew off tweeting with fright—the girl tried to take advantage of the quick surrender of the streets and enter into intimacy with whatever the neighing horses were sensing in the township. But the only means of contact was looking and she saw the soldiers on the corner. Ah, the soldiers.

"Just look at the soldiers, Perseu," said Lucrécia.

Her way of seeing was crude, hoarse, clipped: the soldiers! But she wasn't the only one seeing. In fact a man was passing by and looked at her: she had the feeling he'd seen her narrow and elongated, with a too-small hat: as in a mirror. She batted her eyelids disturbed, though she didn't know what shape she'd choose to have; but whatever a man sees is a reality. And without realizing it the girl took the shape that the man had perceived in her. That's how things were built. She turned all modest toward Perseu—like an elongated person—reaching out, removing a bit of lint from his jacket. She investigated Perseu's face, looking at him insistently as the man who'd walked by would understand what she looked at.

Perseu and Lucrécia stared at each other ...

Perseu then faced the store, not right afterward—trying to move his gaze slowly so as not to take it blatantly off her. He was polite. He even started whistling a bit. But the moment was getting more and more unsustainable, what had happened? she said with humility and dream:

"What a windy day, huh."

The fellow stopped whistling immediately and looked at the day. For no reason he faked a suffocating cough and when at last he got control of it spoke with a certain importance.

"Yeah, huh."

The dog was running down the sidewalk with weak paws, trotting, wagging its tail in light. Perseu awkwardly frightened it off—his beardless face smiling out of shame and delight at being such a coward. Big, polite. He could have grown his hair out, full of curls; he knew how to make verses and was Catholic:

"So big and afraid of a dog," she said rudely looking him over with curiosity and the street organ on the corner began to play Toselli's Serenade heating up the street. The musician was turning the crank and the machine was swallowing the music with difficulty and care—the music was taking on several quick object-like shapes ... would everything that tumbled into that city materialize into a thing? then the girl stopped and grabbed her purse from the ground. Perseu tried out of revenge to show that he was well aware that she walked around with a purse full of useless things, wilted flowers from the dance, papers; he tried with wisdom to show at least that he was seeing because one couldn't even understand it.

But when Lucrécia lifted her head from the ground, light was emerging from her hair ... some thing turning around and showing its good side; her eyes, disappointed for a second, were releasing the same empty light as her hair, and stopped looking in order to allow themselves to be seen: Perseu tried quickly at least to see. Also from the girl's stained lips a breath of brightness was being born ... whatever she possessed was slipping through fingers—so lovely ... she looked like she didn't bathe, her nails and neck of a dubious color, standing in the air—so lovely, he thought desperately, so lovely ... she seemed blind.

"I really like you!" the fellow said stubbornly, his forehead lowered to charge.

She turned around with harshness and extreme joy:

"You know I don't like that sort of thing!" she said coquettishly, taking offense.

Perseu looked at her ashamed laughing, and she started to laugh too. And they laughed so much that they choked for real or were faking it and started coughing. Lucrécia Neves had stopped and was wiping her eyes, red all over, disheveled: he saw quite well ... Oh, loving her was a permanent effort— he stopped serious, bathed by the palest sun, peering into the distance with dissatisfaction. The young man's eyes were open. His pupils dark and golden. There was a solitude forever in the way he was standing. Then she said:

"Let's go," she said sweetly also because she was already starting to cheat on him.

At the stairs of the house where the girl lived, he said he'd wait for her to go up.

"No," she answered all intimate and scheming, "I'm the one waiting for you to go, understand …", she was speaking with great politeness trembling all over in her hat but looking him in the eye with concern: she didn't want the trouble of going upstairs just to come back down. But he laughed extraordinarily flattered:

"Well then, farewell!"

"Salutations," she said suffocating with laughter.

The fellow blushed:

"Salutations," he said without looking at her. He went off slowly trying to be elegant in Lucrécia's eyes but you could tell he'd lost his natural way of walking. The girl watched him wave in relief as he turned onto the first street. She herself answered by moving her fingers above her hat. Then she stopped smiling, dried up, inexpressive for a moment. She waited a bit.

She leaned forward until she could see the clock on the column. She was waiting thoughtfully, it was hard to get ready once again. Finally, looking both ways, she went out.

The movement in the streets had calmed down and the afternoon light was sharp and discolored. On the corner the wagon seemed fantastical … the ropes and wheels in a breath of light. The girl's face was moving ahead gently, watchful. You could already even glimpse the stone square full of hitched horses. Next to the column with the clock she stood waiting. With her thoughts blind and calm due to the kind of light.

The people in the distance were already black. And between the flagstones the strips of earth were dark. Lucrécia Neves was waiting, aerial, peaceful. Adjusting without looking the straps of her dress. The square. What a sight. What a threshold. She didn't cross it. The cooler air was turning her hands white and the girl seemed to be rejoicing at that: she'd glance at them now and then, precise. Above the shops the same insignificant and unmistakable expression that belonged to Perseu was wandering—the girl recognized it: it was São Geraldo at dusk. She was waiting.

The township too, at that hour, had reached its final stage. It would now be impossible to replace a door, a lamppost. Or the equestrian statue. Or one of the impersonal men who were passing by without touching the ground. The panting of the horses was making life precious all around … Standing upright might knock off balance the girl who'd shift the position of her feet from time to time: she too with a superficial sensitivity that in another inwardly turned second was becoming unreachable; sometimes she'd touch her hair and tremble shivering at herself, the motionless horses would beat their hooves for a second on the colorless stone. The girl's face wasn't saying anything. Her mouth hard, delicate. It was the end of the day.

Eventually Felipe showed up in his uniform, his face red. The closer he came in the light, the more impossible it became to look at him. Until getting close and she no longer seeing him, he became a warrior. She shook his hand with the shyness that the distance between their meetings had created. But the lieutenant quickly destroyed the girl's submissive unfamiliarity by taking her arm, invisible such that she wasn't looking, he almost mute, such that she was already hardly hearing:

"My beauty in blue, let's go see the water right away since I have to go to bed early, tomorrow is a training day. And to top it off this devil of a horse is giving up."

That's how a man spoke. And Lucrécia smiled with displeasure and polite lividness, already possessed by the light of the township. She let herself be monotonously led once more through the Gate toward the stream he was calling water—behind the railroad. Where they'd sit on the rock. Felipe was talking and asking questions invisible, the girl guessing that he'd twist his neck now and then, in a gesture that would give him great beauty and extra-human freedom: a new habit of his after he'd finally been admitted to the cavalry; and she was also trying to imitate him with watchfulness, imitating a horse. After he'd changed weapons, everything that was bothering him was easily chased off, Lieutenant Felipe now looked like he was always on horseback. That's how he'd lead the girl away from people, both of them riding the same steed through the ever more invisible crowd. That familiar and distant being, that outsider quick on the draw, well then a warrior! with mild sleepiness the girl was enjoying the company of a lieutenant. If the soldier had so desired, Lucrécia Neves would bind herself to him, if not out of love, at least out of a limitless admiration to which she was susceptible, sinking into whatever sweetness and listening she had inside her—for that was her nature. But the lieutenant didn't want that, he was free. And just as the girl had never truly looked at him, afraid to muddy such a clear surface, he too almost hadn't looked at her because he didn't know her; later, each would forget the other's useless features.

"Damned things!" said Felipe with a twisted mouth kicking the stone that happened to be there.

And she suddenly happy, frightened. Felipe's nose had turned pale with anger. The thing the girl loved most in the lieutenant was the foaming rage into which he could fall.

Damned things! he said again. And turning around with gallantry: "let's go see the water, my beauty." But she was still rejoicing looking toward the hill in the pasture where only at night the beasts would raise their manes in a neigh: damned things! They advanced into the vast tarnished light and there was the water.

Dead things abutted the cliffs. They stood watching. Felipe was smoking. But each nearby thing was distant for the girl, she only had her eyes. She herself out of reach.

And that's how the city was at that hour.

The land around the water was full of humus, fecund, exhaling—Lucrécia Neves was breathing it in with impotence and delicateness. From staring at the stream for so long her face had fastened to one of the rocks, floating and becoming warped in the current, the only spot that was hurting, barely hurting from floating and dreaming so much in the water. Eventually she wasn't sure if she was looking at the image or if the image was staring at her because that's how things had always been and you couldn't be sure if a city had been made for the people or the people for the city—she was looking.

When Felipe stirred she remembered with a start his presence to her left ... quickly she raised her left shoulder until it touched her ear, protecting herself from the lieutenant with wounded sweetness. She thought, almost awakening and perking up her ears, she thought the foreigner would say: what filth! she almost heard him blaspheme and again leaned her shoulder against her ear, recoiled, hunched. She was full of free rancor, the stream was metallic, and a bird flew over the dirty waters! her shoulder was stroking her ear like a wing, dislodging her hat, the wind blowing over the city of steel. But Felipe was tying his shoelaces whistling in the brightness, and saying nothing. Whatever he wasn't saying ended up lost in the immense and bluish twilight. The girl then started listening to the soldier's melodious whistling.

Until one more tone sank into the evening. Everything now was in profile, the eaves of the roofs clipped-out in the void ... She relaxed her shoulder, interrupting immediately the quick face-washing the whistling had made so intimate. Now she was sitting up straight: but not a sound could be heard: a weak light was lit in the air.

And little by little, as if they'd fallen asleep, it got very late, and transformed.

Things were growing with deep tranquility. São Geraldo was displaying itself. She standing facing the bright world. Felipe was talking with lost sound ... Even the noises of the township were arriving dismantled in a pale round of applause. The girl was looking while standing, constant, with her patient falcon-like existence. Everything was incomparable. The city was a manifestation. And on the bright threshold of the night all of a sudden the world was the orb. On the threshold of the night, an instant of muteness was the silence, appearing was an appearance, the city a fortress, victims were offerings. And the world was the orb.

In this new universe, an abyss away, there on the ground was the screw.

Lucrécia Neves was looking from her own height at the horror of the object. Terrible and delicate things were resting on the ground. The perfect screw. The girl was inhaling the leaden odor of the brightness. And turning around—there was São Geraldo: annunciated, inexplicable, set down with the hardness of a foot. Each object hyperphysical. The spots. The girl softly moved her hooves.

One more tone sank. Now, in the darkened color of the air, each tower, each smokestack suddenly straightened up ... Now would be the time to disembark and at last touch all things. Would the city let you grope, frightened, its stone? before closing in on the bold prey, raising its walls with one more slab ...

"... what time is it ..." she asked politely.

Felipe scratched his neck, lifting his illuminated chin:

"The same time it was yesterday at this hour ..."

Lucrécia Neves laughed, her dry lips opened with ardor in several bloodless gashes. The girl moistened her lips with her long bird tongue, looking both ways, instinctive, suspicious. Standing, beside the darkened waters, the lieutenant and the girl were growing weaker and weaker beneath the extreme brightness of the city. The township was rising as high as it could go. The light didn't seem to sink but to rise, with stifling effort, to the light. With this effort São Geraldo had become extraordinarily exterior, the stones weightless. Things were staying on their own surface with the vehemence of an egg. Immunized. From afar the houses were hollow and tall.

The cylindrical tower of the power plant.

If this were a world of heroes what a terrifying profile it would have.

"No, really, Felipe darling, what time is it," the girl purred anxious and attractive.

But when São Geraldo would appear, it would appear identical to itself, without revealing itself.

"Didn't I already tell you?" the lieutenant said again examining her in the greenish shadow with greater interest.

She laughed a lot, tossing her empty head with grace and fear, lightly tapping him on his uniform ... the twilight widened then, a rapier had been driven trembling into the air! the color of the girl's dress suddenly paled with wilting, the straps trembled, the bracelets sank in purple insignias ... São Geraldo was barely standing.

"Let's go," said Felipe, and the man's voice was ringing out like pushing off branches, and like steps.

They started walking once again toward the center of town. The surfaces thinning out more and more though inside each thing it was still dark and shining.

Another moment however — and a flower suddenly drooped on its stem, roots sweetened in the rotting earth, the substructures of the houses were tumbling down — the whole city was trembling after having collapsed.

The danger had passed. It was night.

All that remained was the immediate echo of the stone, a brightening in the man passing by. A light turning on in the already nocturnal air that smelled of bread ... And now a pleasant externality of old root. But everything again untouchable. The world was indirect.

Lucrécia was worn-out and innocent, Lieutenant Felipe was looking at the clouds with precision without seeing them. And finally they turned onto the street that would take them to the center. The township had darkened and lit up like a ship. Right now it was invisible ... you could only see the odd streetlamp and the small lit-up areas. The rest were bastions in darkness. Lucrécia was walking with dreamy security in the company of a soldier. He was smiling a bit, the horseman, observing her aslant. In order to say at last, so pleasant and happy — he seemed to come from a meadow where he'd been running free:

"Why are you so selfish and won't give me a kiss!"

Forgetting to not look at him, the girl saw him close-up—now invisible again because he was so close. She breathed the almost-night air. The smell of warm flour in the streets and her mother waiting to have dinner on a second floor. How dark it was getting.

Almost cheery, finally shredding the slender veins of the night, the girl stood on her hooves, breathed deeply releasing her battle cry—and when he was near, touchable on his buttons—stabbable—she mumbled, gradually losing the use of speech:

"Never!" she said laughing unpleasant in her glory, in her useless cry of conquest that came from São Geraldo, "never! I'll bite you, that's right, Felipe … Felipe!" she called in the darkness, "I'll walk all over you, that's the kiss you'll get!" she said already serious, completely focused on her feet that were stomping.

Felipe opened his mouth in fright. And that's how they stood looking at each other, astonished, curious, increasingly shivering. Finally he gave a fake laugh, trying to free his neck:

"You've got no manners at all!"—a child running unleashed crossed between them—"And it's my fault for hanging around people of this sort, these must be the manners of this filthy township of yours!" he said now with pleasure, insulting her right in her city.

Both recoiled opening a small clearing, bristling, moving about, cautious. In the shadows the lieutenant was almost laughing out of rage. The girl would never laugh, pale. At the same time she could suddenly do a somersault in the air.

That's what the young man seemed to foresee and recoiled even more. And finally after a bit of effort he turned his back.

Lucrécia trembled enormous raising herself on her tiptoes: this outsider would never leave victorious. That new and painful inspiration, like water entering her nose, and she splashing her large animal body in order to keep afloat:

"Look!"

She still didn't know what she was going to say but it was urgent, it was a question of fighting for the kingdom. She saw the young man turn around with hope—at that distance the uniform was shining beautifully, lost, his loveliest object. And Lucrécia Neves looked at it disappointed.

The street was blinking with darkness and light. Hesitant figures of girls were starting to move about along the walls, searching. The women of the city. The smell of the invisible stones of the houses and the nausea of the gas burners were mingling in the new wind—the girl saw herself years back running to get bread for dinner, flying between the last people of the night, terrorized by the dark form of the hill, she herself frightening as she ran ...

"Look!" she said. "Why don't you kiss your grandmother, she's not from São Geraldo!" she finally threw at him, tragic, out loud so everyone could hear.

It was horrible, and she was shaking all over in the darkness. While the embarrassed lieutenant was twisting his neck and adjusting the uniform insulted in public—someone had stopped in the shadow of the sidewalk smiling with great interest. It had been the meeting of two horses in the air, both dripping with blood. And they wouldn't stop until one was king. She had wanted him because he was an outsider, she hated him because he was an outsider. The fight for the kingdom. Lucrécia Neves elbowed the woman who was watching eliciting a small cry of fright. She violently straightened her hat, shaking her bracelet in the air. And with her head high, holding back a dizziness that would make her fly over the smokestacks — she took her leave slowly, full of trembling ribbons.

She was all worked up, now and then she'd give a kick with one of her hind legs at her absent tail. But as she was crossing the street, unable to wait any longer she started to tell herself what had happened, in detail; she had hard eyes and lips dripping with saliva while recounting: "then I said to darling Felipe: only a criminal would dare!" Oh, Perseu, she suddenly murmured turning her thoughts to the one who'd never offend her.

But Perseu dressed like a farmhand. And the girl was already needing, in her iron streets, the armed forces.

She arrived at Market Street when it was already dark. She kept examining herself anxious as if she might be shredded. And losing the lieutenant … And he'd be Captain someday! … Oh, oh, Felipe! she called.

I'm fooling them all, I don't want anything, she thought with spite clinging to the lights that the lamplighter was brightening. But in a general way she liked men so much. Oh, Felipe, she said with regret.

What frightened her, as she passed the closed butcher shop, is that no one was talking about marrying her. Only Mateus who respected her with paternal and ceremonious desire, visiting her mother in order to win the daughter. Which was already beginning to appeal to her, it all had a familiar and repugnant air, it reeked in short of what people call real life. Mateus who'd watch her while smoking a cigar. With him, she'd have a luxurious and violent future … The girl really was eager to marry.

Ah, some news, some news, she suddenly asked in agony, oh, to find at last at home a messenger from afar, his clothes dusty, suitcases in the hallway, and who'd take out a letter from his leather satchel. And while her mother was serving the stranger a glass of liqueur, she'd open the letter trembling, the letter that would take her far away!

Because São Geraldo was asphyxiating her with its mud and its cloves floating in the gutters.

Ana had turned on the feeble lights and was waiting in the lounge chair for dinner. She was the only spectator. The house immersed in the silence of electricity.

And right there was her room.

Like a piano left open. How frightening to see things. The design of the beams in the ceiling was strange and new, like that of a hanging chair … She took off her shoes while looking up, put away her hat while smoothing it out, counting on the unforeseeable day of tomorrow. Suddenly straightening herself.

She grabbed a handkerchief, covered her nose. The handkerchief came back wet with blood. She leaned her head back as she'd been taught. Taking advantage to look at the ceiling beams. The liquid was running warmly and the room smelled of blood. She stayed like that, without impatience, panting a bit. Her mouth muted by the cloth, her eyes enlarged. At last she removed the handkerchief. Between her nose and her mouth the blood had dried giving her face a filthy and childish appearance. Once again she'd come back wounded.

Ugly, wilted beneath her disheveled hair, sniffing occasionally; the haunting had passed and she'd returned to the great frogs. But she also remained whole—fighting without wearing out, she was horrible, the patriot.

She took off her dress and, sweating in the slip stuck to her body, breathed with closed eyes. Her hair was hiding half of her struck face. Lucrécia Neves was wiping her forehead with the back of her hand as if she'd taken a beating, comforting herself as best she could. She was dirty and bloody. Snorting humiliated while stroking her ear with her shoulder.

4   The Public Statue

THE STEPS TO THE DINING ROOM WERE THREE AND the difference in height threw the room into some relief. The township's poor electricity, in those days distributed only to a few houses, would construct at night a compartment full of structures and cores where the ticktack of the pendulum would tumble down precisely — concentric circles erasing themselves in the shadows of the furniture. Yellowing tea cozies, the little stuffed bird, the wooden box with an Alpine landscape on the lid, were Ana's meticulous presence.

The house seemed decorated with the spoils of a bigger city.

"You're tired," Ana asked from the head of the table, squinting her eyes as if her daughter were far away and the light between them strong.

Lucrécia didn't like this room so permeated with Ana's happy widowhood. To understand it a continuity of presence would be required, the girl seemed to be thinking trying to look at each object: they'd reveal nothing and reserve themselves only for her mother's way of looking. Her mother who'd move them around and dust them — then take a step back, as if sculpting them, in order to examine them from afar with myopic delicateness—a sideways gaze. The objects themselves now could only be seen obliquely; a straight-on stare would see them cross-eyed. After examining them Ana would sigh and stare at Lucrécia signaling that she was now available; Lucrécia would divert her eyes toward the ceiling, rude.

Ana was increasingly trying to get closer, anxious to convey to her the insignificant secrets that were suffocating her: in fact she was already complaining of not sleeping at night. Lucrécia would divert her eyes.

She'd been solitary for a while now, and loving that widowhood without the shocks that can come from a man, the woman was nonetheless starting to worry—and trying to drag her daughter toward an intimacy in which both might construct sneaky compensations, sighs and delights, that pleasure of a seamstress at her sewing, Ana who'd rejoice when there was some article of clothing to mend.

Uselessly she was seeking her daughter's support asking her with her patient gaze for the sacrifice. What the sacrifice might consist of, neither needed to know: but Ana was asking, Lucrécia turning her down—and secondary requests and denials were emerging, unimportant in themselves but enormous in the dining room, loaded with the same stubbornness: why didn't Lucrécia spend the evenings with her in the dining room?

But if the girl finally gave in—the room and Ana, radiant, were encircling her, the teacups sparkling, the Alpine landscape in extraordinary prominence, nothing however capable of being seen straight-on—though Ana would try to teach her to see from the perspective of beauty, pointing out here and there:

"The china cabinet looks much nicer with my little bird on

the first shelf, you can see it much better, right, sweetie," she'd say.

But it was just a way of seeing, and nothing more.

And when Lucrécia was in the living room, which was called "resting after dinner, mama"—the door might open and Ana would turn up with a mischievous smile, carrying her bag of yarn, needles and embroidery frames: ready to visit her. The girl however revealed nothing to her. Ana would sit ceremonious and dreamy without unrolling her needlework—looking with some curiosity at the trinkets, the small table, this living room that because it rarely received visits had become her daughter's second bedroom. Left to herself, Ana Rocha Neves would eventually start speaking of her youth, with details that would suffocate her if she didn't transmit them with exactness: she'd sometimes stop for a long while until making up her mind precisely when some fact had happened. And thinking she was speaking of herself, she'd only describe the place where she'd lived when she left the farm until finding a husband:

"Now that, that was a city, sweetie, and not this hole: even the horses had bells, and a church was a church, a house was a house, a street was a street—not this hole with houses that don't even make sense."

Despite the details, what a lost city that had been, and what a mixed-up youth! her mother had been happy and scared in her city, that was it in the end. And when the revolution was over, the silence had frightened her, she'd gone to sleep in her sister's bed.

That was the thing that alarmed Lucrécia Neves about the story. The girl too seemed to be familiar with this fear that wasn't fear, just getting chills down the spine in the face of a thing. Once she'd gone to the state museum and been afraid of having a wet umbrella in a museum. That's what had happened. She was afraid of seeing, in a single glance, a train and a little bird. And of a man with a diamond ring on his middle finger: Mateus. She'd freeze if that finger pointed her out.

Also with a movement of hers in bed a crippled and content being would sometimes take shape in the roses on the wall— then she'd shiver the way a dog barks at a wardrobe.

Worried by the silence, Ana stirred at the head of the table, passing her the bread plate. But the girl looked at her.

And then the game started up again. Lucrécia Neves removed the slice and placed it decisively on the table, without touching it.

This stupidity had one day been the opening scene of a long conversation about a lack of appetite that ended in accusations of love and sadness, and had become the secret starting signal. Ana immediately received the short message. She answered her with enormous eyes fixed on the plate: which was already feigned. Something had begun. The two women became sly and shrewd, running cautiously like rats through the shadowy room—and taking on the unfamiliar natures of two characters they'd never know how to describe but could imitate, just by imitating themselves.

That was when a soft and singing rain started to fall, the wind opened the window. Ana, impatient with the interruption, got up to shut it, and the whole room became more interior: both trembled with pleasure, exchanged a glance of friendship.

"Today I got so tired, I even felt like I was going to die," Lucrécia began with a decisive sigh.

"Is that so?" said her mother making an effort so Lucrécia would notice her interest through the ceremonious tone she'd adopt when they were beginning a "scene." "Isn't that something!" she added a bit foolish, feigning a special understanding.

But this time a certain sadness overtook that woman who, a bit dreamy, was stroking her fork. She was even almost smiling. At other times, when her daughter would touch her, Ana would jump startled and still try to trot amidst the things. But today she was slightly panting. "Is that so?" she repeated tilting a face to which some thought of calm desperation gave an expression of such luminous love that if anyone saw it that person would have seen love.

The certainty of a great experience, despite her reclusive life, overtook this more-than-mature woman. She looked with some compassion at that girl across from her, full of stupid youth, whom you could never teach … teach … kindness? what kindness? she'd have to learn all by herself.

"Isn't that something!" said Ana Rocha Neves disappointed.

The girl then answered that if she died—"anyway what did it matter? mother wouldn't even cry."

If they were awakened, maybe they'd be surprised that, with such scarce resources, they could fall so completely into their roles. But they no longer needed much preparation to get into character, and the beginnings were getting quicker every time, almost impatient.

"Mother wouldn't cry," Lucrécia said, and this offended Ana. It had become clear, amidst the sheets of rain, that if the woman wouldn't cry, Lucrécia wasn't the one who would lose out—for in that moment she'd be the one who was humble and dead.

The girl continued: "you wouldn't even have to cry just like Perseu for example didn't cry" … Ana agreed quickly avenging herself on the fellow who'd stolen from her so many of her daughter's hours.

But, by agreeing that Perseu wouldn't cry, she'd accepted one of the facts of the pronouncement — and the comparison itself became impossible to contradict. The woman fell silent while Lucrécia was gaining strength and a certain bitterness for having convinced her so easily. Experience should have taught her that there was no point waiting for her mother to object. Above all the role that had fallen to Ana seemed to have an even weaker character than the real one.

"Because you'd be alone, you wouldn't even need to pay for my clothes, mama, and if you missed being around people you could even find some girlfriends …"

Ana was now almost smiling at the hopes Lucrécia had given to her; and with troubled eyes, eyes already immersed in the future, she was almost agreeing.

"And you could marry Perseu's father …" she continued now horrified imagining that sanguine man scorning her dear mama. She'd never gone that far and both looked at each other surprised. The woman finally stirred in her chair, flushed:

"Well now, young lady! …" — she said coquettishly.

Lucrécia was afraid and added cautiously:

"Or, don't then, mama dear, just live more comfortably …"

Ana nodded quickly in agreement — for a short instant she looked at and away from her daughter, smiling suspiciously.

But faced with Ana's contented gaze the girl couldn't stand it anymore, and some thing finally breaking, out of tune, she swallowed her food, got up running and was kneeling beside her mother who was staring at her terrified and blushing with pleasure …

"… mama how sad our life is!" she cried smothered by the woman's legs. (What about the dances, what about the dances? the devil was saying to her.) Ana babbled something, full of modesty, offended: "I don't think so!" she was mumbling almost haughty.

But while she kept her suffocated expression, and the whole room that she wasn't seeing was spinning dizzily, the girl seemed to discover that she hadn't cried out because of sadness. It was because she could no longer bear that mute existence that was always above her, the room, the city, the high degree the things atop the china cabinet had reached, the small dry bird ready to fly, stuffed, around the house, the height of the tower of the power plant, so much intolerable balance—that only a horse could manage to express with rage atop its hooves. So much joy that would never be broken—and that only sometimes the military band would burst finally making all the city's windows open.

When the girl stood her face was tranquil.

Things were perched around her, very calm. Coffee cups were steaming, her mother seated, table and tablecloth, everything unconquerable once again.

She sat to drink her coffee. Maybe she was thinking how burlesque their lives would be if they spoke to each other? and how São Geraldo would be destroyed if, instead of watching it keeping it beyond the reach of the voice—someone finally spoke. If she and Ana had talked, she'd have so often before broken resistance itself with a sincerity. But among people without intelligence there was no need to explain yourself.

"Ah, Lucrécia, oh my daughter, I haven't slept well," Ana said forsaken by the independence of Lucrécia, whom the quick surrender no longer seemed to alter.

"Dear mama, you need to get out of the house a bit more."

"God forbid, darling daughter, ah, my God."

Before Ana could go on, tying her down for a long conversation, the girl stood, crossed the hallway and entered the living room. Where the lights of other houses were making it pointless to turn on the lamp. She then grabbed the pair of shoes and started shining them slowly in the half-light.

At first a bit unrecognizable, after an instant the room was regaining its old position having as its center the flower. The spirit was the wind, the northwesterly wind was blowing insistently, broken by the houses on the street.

The room was replete with pitchers, trinkets, chairs and crocheted doilies, and cluttering the floral-papered walls were cut-out pages of magazines and old calendars. The suffocated and pure air of forever closed-off places, the smell of things. But would the auction soon begin and the objects be put on display? nothing would really keep the door from opening— the wind was foreshadowing doors roughly thrown ajar.

Rubbing the shoes more slowly, the daydreaming girl was examining with pleasure her fortress, not peeking at it but looking at it straight on: she was getting ready to face things with loyalty. Remaining perched just as on the hill in the pasture— that's how she was looking around. In this girl, who knew little more of herself than her own name, the effort to see was the effort to give herself outward expression. The mason building the house and smiling with pride—everything that Lucrécia Neves could know of herself was outside her: she was seeing.

Courage however was deciding to start. As long as she didn't begin, the city was intact. And it would be enough to start looking to smash it into a thousand pieces that she could never put back together afterward.

It was a patience of constructing and demolishing and constructing again and knowing she might die one day right when she'd demolished in the process of building.

Amidst her ignorance she'd only felt that she needed to start with the first things of São Geraldo—with the living room—thus remaking the whole city. She'd even planted the first stake of her kingdom looking at: a chair. All around however the void had continued. Not even she herself could draw near to that created area that a chair had made unapproachable. She'd never been able to go beyond the serenity of a chair and head toward second things.

Though, while she was looking, had some time passed that would one day be called perfecting? those long years that were passing through scattered moments: through rare instants Lucrécia Neves possessed a single destiny. Since she was slow, things by dint of being anchored were gaining their own shape with definition—that was what she'd sometimes manage: to reach the object itself.

And to be enthralled: because behold the table in the dark. Raised above itself by its lack of function. The other things of the room engorged by their own existence, whereas anything that at least wasn't solid, like the small hollow three-legged table—didn't have, didn't give—was transitory—surprising—perched—extreme.

Telegram signals. Behold the raised shape of the small table. When a thing didn't think, the form it had was its thought. The fish was the fish's only thought. What about the smokestack. Or that small page of the calendar that the wind left trembling … Ah, yes, Lucrécia Neves was seeing everything.

Though she gave nothing of herself—except for the same incomprehensible clarity. The secret of things was in that, by showing themselves, they showed themselves exactly as they were.

That's how it was. And rubbing her shoe, the girl looked at this dark world replete with trinkets, the flower, the single flower in the vase: this was the township—she was polishing furiously.

Behold the flower—showing its thick stem, the round corolla: the flower was showing off. But atop the stem it too was untouchable, the indirect world. No point being motionless: the flower was untouchable. When it started to wilt, you could now look at it directly but by then it would be too late; and after it died, it would become easy: you could throw it away touching it all over—and the room would shrink, you'd wander among diminished things with firmness and disappointment, as if whatever was mortal had died and the rest were eternal, without danger.

Ah, ah, the familiar air of the room was vibrating. Ah, the girl with four shoes was watching. The desire to go to a dance would sometimes emerge, grow and leave sea-foam on the beach. Shoes in hand Lucrécia Neves twisted her head and sneakily tried to peer at the living flower. She even came closer, sniffed it warily. She grew dizzy from breathing so deeply, the flower itself growing dizzy from being breathed in—it was giving itself! But once a certain moment arrived,—the sudden blow of the hoof!—and the fragrance became impenetrable. There was the exhausted flower yet with the same amount of fragrance as before … What was the flower made of if not of flower itself.

That's how it was. And beside her, the porcelain boy playing the flute. A sober thing, dead, as fortunately could never be imagined.

Oh, but things were never seen: people were the ones who saw.

And nearby the solid door of the room. And farther beyond the porcelain woman was bearing on her back the small stopped clock.

All this was the miniature version of the church, the square and the clock tower, and on this map the young woman was making calculations like a general. So what would she say if she could go, from seeing objects, to saying them … That was what she, with the patience of a mute, seemed to desire. Her imperfection came from wanting to say, her difficulty in seeing was like that of painting.

The hard thing is that appearance was reality.

Now the rain was falling in great sheets.

Meanwhile some time had passed. And if nothing had been transformed, the night already had lost its date, and was smelling of moist whitewash.

The girl opened the magazine distractedly, and in the dark could barely make out the figures. But there were the Greek statues … Could one of them be pointing? … but it no longer had an arm. And they'd even displaced it from the spot that it was indicating with the remaining piece of marble; each one should stay in his own city because, transported, he would point to the void, such was the freedom of travel. There was the piece of marble. In the dark. What a sight! the girl put down the magazine, got up—what would she do until getting married? except walk back and forth—and she opened the doors of the balcony with curiosity.

She'd hardly cracked the doors when the great night entered with the wind throwing them ajar—but after the first gust you only felt the pulsing of the darkness, the lights of the street almost erased beneath the rain.

On the corner a wagon with a lit lamp was dragging along, spurred on. When the wheels vanished in the distance nothing more was heard.

There was the city.

Its possibilities were terrifying. But it never revealed them! Only every once in a while a glass would shatter.

If at least the girl were outside its walls. What a painstaking work of patience it would be to encircle it. To waste her life trying geometrically to lay siege to it with calculations and resourcefulness in order to one day, even when she was decrepit, find the breach.

If at least she were outside its walls.

But there was no way to besiege it. Lucrécia Neves was inside the city.

The girl leaned out, listening, looking, ah, rain with wind, her calm blood was saying, she was leaning, listening, ah! Lucrécia was breathing, breaking off her encounter with the great darknesses beyond the Gate: it must have been raining upon the deserted tracks.

You could even make out the bathed lights of the station. On the hill in the pasture, in the storm, what would the wet horses be doing?

The bolts of lightning opening clearings and illuminating for a second the dripping coat, the pupils dangerous with humiliation. The equines! then the thunderclaps rolling patiently and closing the hill in darkness. Lucrécia Neves's face was making an effort, curious, beyond its own figure, listening. But you could only hear the streets flowing with rain ...

Leaning then on the blinds she murmured: ah, I'd love to have the strength of a window, she murmured to herself quietly, and through these words she was perhaps disguising other older words, seeking a lost rite. Inexplicably more hopeful, she was now trying to provoke her wrath until reaching her own strength, trotting watchfully, venturing to touch the objects— until happening upon whatever would be the key to things, touching the door with a delicate hand and with a serenity that this too would never burst its own limit—such was the extraordinary balance everything was keeping.

Some news, she thought with other words, outdoing herself in new rage—and listening hopefully: but the night, the night encircling the clock tower was the reply.

She advanced slumbering, yawning furiously without self-delusion, sniffing up close the smell of chairs, the smell the wind was lifting and scattering—she was already disheveled as if from rough work. Come to me, she essayed while blushing … A new burst of thunder rolled with sadness, the girl purred with pleasure. Come to me, she said with other words. Not even she herself answered. The rain was singing in pipes.

Yawning she kneeled before the sofa, sank her face into the cushion: she'd always rest after dinner.

And the mustiness coming from the furnishing's well-cared-for old age.

Yet I've been patient, she thought running her fingers over the ridges of the leather; her patience came from so many walks and brimmed hats.

The news, she was making an effort, empty. The motionless horses in the rain. Ah, she said with rage and humility, her sleepy hands braiding a lock of hair.

She didn't know where to start hoping again, the room covered her in a wave, but she kept her eyes open inside the cushion, a severed head in the Museum: she was dreaming curious in the dark, the horses were advancing on the hill, the positions of the game were switched.

That's when she heard steps on the sidewalk.

Trying one more time to pay attention, she started hearing them on the stairs.

They were getting closer. The girl was waiting with her

narrow intelligence, her senses on edge. Her left shoulder was stroking her ear slyly, her head in the cushion … Finally the steps halted near the room. With difficulty hearing, Lucrécia Neves invented hearing the door creak.

She paused, the ostrich feather in her hand and the half-written page on the desk. Trying one more time to invent something, and her hand was resting on wide skirts. She leaned her pale face forward now framed by two plaits of hair: her aspect was ennobled by patience. With the raised feather in her hand, she finally looked. The door was opening and the wind was penetrating making the room waver. A man appeared and water was streaming down his cape. When she thought he'd never speak, the visitor said above his drenched beard:

"It's here, Lucrécia. The ship's already here."

For the first time they were pronouncing her name emphasizing her destiny.

It was a name to be called from afar, then from nearer by, until they handed her the letter, breathless. She took her handkerchief from one of her cuffs, covering her mouth with the lace to hide her trembling:

"Well-laden?"

The man looked with a certain hesitation.

"Always the same. Coal. Always coal."

Lucrécia Neves remained rigid.

"You can go then," she said to him with eyes full of cold tears, "you can go, it doesn't matter."

That wasn't the shipment, that wasn't the news! The large man was blocking the doorway. He looked like he might topple over, and the girl wondered if he might be wounded. But the man was now staring forcefully at the trinkets, and without a smile despising the fresh whiteness of the porcelain.

"It's coal," he repeated shrugging with irony, "it's coal …"

"Go away," she ordered firmly.

The door finally closed. Lucrécia Neves rested the quill atop the desk and grew thoughtful.

Blinking inside the cushion.

Oh, she'd been free to invent the news she was awaiting and yet had sought once again with her freedom fateful things, such was the balance. The night was heavy with rain.

The girl finally lifted her head from the sofa and looked out all drowsy. Under the water the living room was floating before eyes that had just arrived from the darkness. The trinkets were gleaming in a brightness of their own like deep-sea animals. The room was intimate, fantastic, the interior suffocated with dreaming ... Throughout the chamber innocent things were scattered keeping a lookout.

The girl's face too was brutalized and sweet. Her body could barely support her heavy head.

She rose sleepily to the window, and in fact, just as she was touching the sill, she heard the sound of wings. From the invisible balcony next door the dove rose terrified amidst the rain and flying off disappeared.

As if the wing had struck her face, with her heart beating awakened: "it even looked like the dove had taken off from your hands, just think!" The error of vision went up in a firework, the window opened and slammed down again, the wind crossed the room making it shiver—at the back of the wide-awake house other windows were opening in reply—dryly the blinds kept banging and the whole house was pierced with cold and height: the fragile second floor was shuddering in the wet windows and in the mirrors, and all around the flower large sleepy wasps were fleeing in fright, the intimate horror of the flower was freeing itself in a thousand lives—the township invading the living room in a rhythmic trot? ... The lightning. The chamber was revealing itself in brightness, the porcelain flashing—these things provoked at great length were gleaming in the eye: not that either! she was saying shuddering beneath the mechanism she herself had unleashed. After the lightning the living room went dark.

The rain was running fast dragging antlers and bits of rotten tree trunks.

The girl was looking at the widened corners of the room, trying to clasp the first solid lifeline: she stared at the confused keyhole that beneath her fixed gaze was perfecting itself into a smaller, smaller keyhole, until reaching its own delicate size.

Feeling more lucid, she'd nonetheless lost a certain amount of uncountable time—she who had come so close that for an instant she'd feared being sanctified—by reality? And now she wanted to go ahead but the void was encircling her and in the void the keyhole was grabbing her—she wanted to hoist herself above the keyhole but what a bird's cry of effort it was to hoist herself again, only someone who flew could know how heavy a body was—the living room lit up in a silent flash, closed up calm and throbbing in the dark; the last candle snuffed out. Tranquil thunderclaps resounded beyond the Gate. In the silence the drops were running down the window.

The girl quickly yawned, out of time. She was standing, hunched, humble. Everything seemed to be waiting for her too to stomp firm and fast with her hoof.

And amid incessant yawns she too would have liked to thus express her modest function which was: to look. What an inexpressive living room, she thought from afar chewing her thumbnail. The waters were running to the sewers, liquid, abundant ... The scattered animals were waiting.

An instant when she'd express herself and place herself on the same level as the city. An instant when she'd show herself, and have the shape she needed as an instrument.

Then, austere, she tried with honesty to say. Angrily chewing her nail, she leaned her head forward: as an expression.

But no, nothing had been said … She looked at wood, table, statuette, the true things, trying to perfect herself in imitation of such a palpable reality! but she seemed to be missing, in order to say, greater destiny. The girl was searching for it: leaning her torso forward and scrutinizing herself with hope. But again she'd made a mistake.

So she erased everything and started over. She hoisted herself this time on tiptoe; listened. Surprising herself by discovering, through the freedom of choosing her movements, the hardness of small bones, of irrevocable and delicate little laws: there were gestures you could carry out and others that were prohibited.

She'd fallen into an ancient art of the body and this body was seeking itself out fumbling along in ignorance.

Until seeming to find the simple subtlety of the body, transformed at last into the thing that acts.

So she stretched out one of her hands. Hesitant. Then more insistent. She stretched it out and suddenly twisted it showing her palm. In the movement her shoulder lifted crippled …

But that's really how it was. She stuck out her left foot. Sliding it across the floor, the tips of her toes diagonal to her ankle. She was somehow so twisted that she wouldn't return to her normal position without wreaking havoc on her whole body.

With her palm cruelly exposed, her outstretched hand was asking and at the same time: Pointing. Lifted by such a fast intensity that she balanced on the unmovable—like the flower in the pitcher.

Behold the mystery of an untouchable flower: the rejoicing intensity. What crude art. She'd reduced herself to a single foot and a single hand. The final motionlessness after a leap. She seemed so poorly made.

Expressing with the gesture of the hand, atop the single foot, both gracefully bent in an offering, her only face shaking in pantomime, behold, behold, all of her, terribly physical, one of the objects. Responding at last while awaiting the beasts.

That's how she stayed until, if she'd urgently need to cry out, she wouldn't have been able to; she'd finally lost the gift of speech. Her hand was set against her cheek like the other side of her face.

"You've got too many hands," she even said to herself and, perfecting herself, hid the other hand further behind her back.

Even a single and motionless hand could sometimes make her whole figure have the quivering of fans. Yet judging herself perfect, she sighed and stayed in position.

So humble and irate that she wouldn't be able to think; and that's how she was giving her thought through its only precise form—wasn't that what happened to things?—inventing out of powerlessness a mysterious and innocent sign that could express her position in the city, choosing her own image and through it the image of the objects.

In this first gesture of stone, whatever was hidden was given outward expression with such prominence. Keeping, for its perfection, the same incomprehensible character: the inexplicable rosebud had opened trembling and mechanical into an inexplicable flower.

And that's how she stayed as if they'd set her down. Distracted, without any individuality.

Her art was commonplace and anonymous. Sometimes

she'd make use of the hand that was behind in order to quickly scratch her back. But right afterward she'd freeze.

In that position, Lucrécia Neves could even be transported to the public square. All she was missing was the sun and the rain. So that, covered in moss, she could finally be unnoticed by the inhabitants and finally be seen every day unconsciously. Because that was how a statue belonged to a city.

The rain had let up, the gutters of the house were starting to swallow the waters avidly. Calm, with her face a bit crooked, the young girl was watching.

So futile and weak, so insignificant, making use of the hand that was at her back to fend off a wasp. But without anyone's having forced her to choose the sacrifice, was she losing right then her youth through the symbol of youth? and life through the shape of life, her single hand pointing.

And so it was that from the side, yawning, she looked like the angel who blows on the doors of churches. Between girl and boy, the eye, already blinking with sleep, looking aslant.

Though when three-quarters of her was seen she suddenly gained volume and shadows, delicateness and opulence: a lame seraph.

In fact set down blameless as in a dentist's waiting room.

Until, beneath the softer sound of the waters running in the pipes, her outstretched hand lost its eloquence—and her head emerged from the disaster in a large and unstable form. Which diminished even its solidity.

Then Lucrécia Neves yawned freely so many times in a row that she looked like a madwoman, until breaking off satiated.

And suspicious.

For she was looking herself over now, with plenty of wonder in her gesture, what gesture? the one that had the urgency of a tic—and like a tic was alarming due to its indomitable mechanical aspect: she even feared being forced to do it in front of other people ... She imagined herself putting down a cup of coffee, standing up sleepily, only later making herself comfortable, relieved—in front of other people.

"This was all a joke, you know," she said to herself with modesty. "This" what, really? She imagined her mother spying on her and closed her eyes in annoyance. She thought of Mateus seeing her passion for trinkets, and through him she didn't understand herself. "So I'm a collector! big deal! you've never seen a collector before?" she answered him rudely. But Mateus didn't put out his cigar and won.

And through him she didn't know herself. Oh, she knew as little about herself as the man did, who, passing by, had looked at her and seen her elongated. And, if she peeked at herself, she'd only see herself as Ana would see her.

Because the truth was: she was a person who was passing on the street, stopping in front of a window display, choosing a pink fabric to admire and saying: it's a color I adore! and people would say: that's Lucrécia Neves's favorite color, and she'd have to explain: but I like other colors too! people would say: I know Lucrécia Neves, she lives at 34 Market Street. She lived on Market Street and this was all a joke, she assured Felipe who knew her so well.

Maybe she'd never find out that she'd foolishly stretched out her hand and foot if, weeks before, she hadn't leaned out of the kitchen window toward the yard behind the store and noticed the cashier of "The Golden Tie."

Without being seen, she'd caught him standing in the sun. Suddenly the man had said pointing to the trash can: "keep quiet, girl." The cashier, standing, noble, was looking at the trashcan with intensity. "Keep quiet, girl," he'd said. Then he'd seemed calm, covered with sadness as if once again a formula had failed.

Without knowing he was being observed, he was entirely intimate and objective. And, so solitary, that it had become impudent to study him. But as he was leaving the yard, he already looked satisfied, even seemed to cover himself with modesty; and traced a gesture that seemed to stop the people's praise. Before entering the store he'd even paused to sniff, adjusting the belt of his pants. And he was laughing mischievously, shaking his shoulders a bit—who inside him was laughing at everyone else? he was skinny, his shoulders stooping in the shirt he was wearing, and, some thing was laughing in him, while he himself—impossible to be interrupted without being thunderstruck—was looking for the last time at the trashcan, sniffing with resentment and satisfaction.

Afraid to rouse him, Lucrécia had withdrawn embarrassed. That same day she'd found him at the bottom of the staircase and he'd said hurried and cordial: good afternoon, Lucrécia.

Made aware of her gesture in the living room, through the memory of the cashier, the girl caught herself starting once more to braid a lock of hair. She almost didn't know what had brought her to such a concrete movement.

What a dirty path was trodden in the darkness until her thoughts burst into gestures! The whole township was working in the underground spaces of the sewers in order for a man here and there to be able to cough on the corner.

In her too the truth was very protected. Which didn't spark much curiosity in her. Just as she'd never needed intelligence, she'd never needed truth; and any picture of her was clearer than she was.

Though, a bit bewildered, she noticed that she knew as much about herself as the cashier in front of the trashcan knew about himself. And, also like him, she took pride in, in such a way, not knowing herself ... "Not knowing herself" couldn't be replaced by "knowing herself."

The girl therefore ended up quite satisfied with the braid between her fingers. If she had any awareness of her gesture, whereas the cashier could never know he'd spoken to a trash can — that was because Lucrécia Neves showed off so much that sometimes she'd even manage to see herself.

Except she'd see herself the way an animal would see a house: no thought going beyond the house.

This was the intimacy without contact that horses had; and the city's houses were entirely seen only by them. And if the lights were gradually going out in the windows, and in the darkness no gaze could express reality any longer — the possible and sufficient sign would be the stomping of the hoof, transmitted from one level to the next until reaching the countryside.

The water was gurgling in the house and inside the living room each clipped-out object was recovering its peaceful existence.

Whatever was made of wood was moist, and the metals icy. The ruins were still steaming. But soon the living room, in its final fumes, was coming to rest in such a way that no one could ever look at it. The last lights turned off.

Though, in the darkness, the girl was still keeping vigil full of sleepiness, dreaming of getting married — the trinket was playing flute in the shadow. One day she'd see the trinket, soon or many years hence, perfection doesn't hurry, a lifetime would be precisely the time of her death. And at least she'd already had her own shape as an instrument of looking: the gesture.

The trinket was playing in the shadow and the girl was moving off with her braid sticking up in the air. She was even seeing the raised flute. But beneath her staring eyes the things started to twist fusing slowly, the flute was doubling until its shapes were beside themselves—thunderstruck by so much watchfulness, Lucrécia Neves nodded off.

The living room, getting ready for the long night, had its eyes open, calm. From afar things are indeterminate—that's how the living room was.

5 In the Garden

A BIT LATER, WHILE SHE WAS CHANGING CLOTHES, LU-
crécia's face was led astray by the first frights of sleep. Haunted
as if she'd already dozed off, she stopped short with her dress
in hand — summoned, weak: a second more and she'd start
to dream. In the bathroom she couldn't even remember what
she'd come looking for. Once more she dragged herself to her
room and stopped at the door.

Across the balcony the wind of the rain was blowing.
Things were exorcized, divided, extremely pale ... the curtain
was flying almost carried off and the room was hesitating as if
someone had just vanished through the window. There was a
moment in the motionlessness of the objects that was haunting in a vision ... In her drowsiness, Lucrécia Neves bristled
when faced with physical things. The light was out. The room
however was lit by the deathly exhalation of each object and
the girl's face itself became touching. To stare at motionless
things for another second lifted her into a sigh of sleep, motionlessness itself transported her into a swoon: yawning cautious, wandering among the objects of the space — childhood
toys spread out over the furniture. A little camel. The giraffe.

The elephant with raised trunk. Ah, bull, bull! crossing the air among the fleshy vegetables of sleep.

Insulted Lucrécia Neves was holding the glass of water she'd brought from the bathroom. She seemed to be hearing through the silence something distant—awake—insistent—unanswerable and urgent.

Soon she was in bed. She fell asleep awake like a candle.

And the night in São Geraldo elapsed clean, astonished.

Ants, rats, wasps, pink bats, herds of mares emerged sleep-walking from the sewers.

What the girl was seeing in her sleep was opening her senses as a house opens at dawn. The silence was funereal, tranquil, a slow alarm that couldn't be rushed. The dream was this: to be alarmed and slow. And also to look at the big things that were coming out from the tops of the houses just as you'd see yourself differently in someone else's mirror: twisted in a passive, monstrous expression.

But the girl's monotonous joy was carrying on beneath the noise of the currents. The dream was unfolding as if the earth weren't round but flat and infinite, and thus there was time. The second floor was keeping her in the air. She was breathing herself out.

The mirror of the room.

But the girl turned her head to the side. Her heart kept beating in the premises. Then the mirror woke her.

She half-opened her eyelids, stared blind. Slowly the things in the room took up their own positions again, recovering their way of being seen by her. Now awake, her consciousness was more demented than her dream, and she was scratching her body with brutish hands.

But soon she kept dreaming through the branches, pushing them away, deaf to advice. Peering foolishly at whatever she was seeing; even remembering the moment itself was unattainable—slow, insensitive, proliferated, she kept going. Searching. Sleep was her maximum attention.

At every halt in the dream, she'd stare at an unknown street with new stones. Even in sleep she was feeling the want of a way of seeing. Attentive, spurred on, she was searching.

All of a sudden on the lane the horses were growing smaller in the distance.

The cry of a locomotive in the station sliced the room with wailing, shaking in her sleep the whole second floor! The girl was touched! amidst the catastrophe, pale inside her carriage, she slept deeper yet.

An already remote whistle made the girl stop short in the dry part of her dream, feeling around with eyes sealed: a number had a certain spot unusable in calculations, the hard bottom: 5721387—this was the number she'd found, bending over to fetch the pebble. Examining it stubborn and inexpressive, giving the dream more difficult moments: turning the pebble over and over.

Until a dog barked on the corner. A barking dog is destiny! Summoned, she immediately tossed away the stone and kept searching without looking back. She was breathing herself out monotonous, symmetrical.

On the headboard the glass of water was shining.

Time was moving on and the night was rotting with crickets and frogs. In the room the air was saturated with the sweetness and love of the late hour.

The girl was searching. Growing older, getting ready for the moment when she'd find it at last.

The delicacy of the objects at rest was starting to fatigue

her, they were already heavy in hands weak with sleep, such a balance hurt so much; and to say that this might only be an instrument! she groaned, scratched her face. And, dragging herself in the dream as best she could, she was now in front of the staircase of the Library, counting the steps.

What wind.

It was patient work to go down and climb up the stairs, to look with nakedness from the top, scanning the dust, testing the landing with her steps or examining it for hours. Finally making up her mind, she started scouring on her knees the stone of the landing. She rubbed the railing of the Library with her sleeve, spat to make it shine.

She was rubbing, forging, polishing, lathing, sculpting, the demented master-carpenter—preparing pale every night the material of the city—and maybe at the very end she'd come to understand—she'd only understand at night—the indirect proof. Scouring the stone with perseverance, leaning from the top with the dishrag in her hand.

She looked closely at a mark the rag would never erase, even embroidered a bit, quickly bought a few things, grabbing the purse that had fallen to the ground ... she was dreaming freely as in a war. Searching.

With packages under her arm she finally went to wait awhile in the stone square, every night that girl would go wait awhile in the stone square, stood beside the equestrian statue in order to wait awhile in the stone square. Over there was the hill in the dark. The dominion of the equines. The girl was looking. She was waiting in the stone square.

Suddenly an urge overcame her, she turned toward the other side of the bed with ferocity—dreamed an instantaneous, hard thing, the hill was sliced with the crooked clarity of a badly-made drawing! ah, ah, the township was breathing itself out full and shivering.

Already running out of time the girl was searching because even at night São Geraldo … — she was hurrying, stumbling on the gratings of the gutters, going deeper into cowardice, into the peaceful alleyways, into her lack of courage to rip up old papers and throw out old dresses, and she was terribly clever about this, hiding in the shadows of the stores, scratching herself radiant with her gloves — breathing extremely agitated, the towers gasping beneath the memory of wars and conquests.

Napoleon's horses were trembling impatiently. Napoleon atop Napoleon's horse was halted in silhouette. Looking ahead in the dark. Behind, all the troops in silence.

But morning didn't come. They waited all night.

Beneath the dream the engines of the township didn't stop, didn't stop, saliva was running from her open mouth.

She finally fell into a deeper sleep. Awake as the moonlight is erect. She was sleeping so deeply that she'd become enormous. Dragging her body, searching.

When she saw the gravel of the stream, she started to hear.

São Geraldo was extremely gentle and buzzing … rotten, peaceful.

Had she searched so much that she'd made a mistake and fallen into a dateless era? even before the first horses. But it was lovely — Lucrécia Neves was clapping her hands with sleepiness, the countryside was lovely! filled with a harmony that was incomparable, able, able, the old destroyed hills were repeating gravely. The echo always had the same insufferable height, traversed by new heights and by new heights … — she making an effort in the only possible way to hear them: remembering them.

The plume was touching with crazed insistence her ear ... the intimate engines weren't stopping. For an instant, the breathed-out sounds became infantile, touched by the same virgin mouth. And now out of tune—an open mouth singing without ecstasy, with a loyal destination; singing from yet before the things.

Or was it just her breathing? sometimes Lucrécia Neves was well aware it was just her breathing filling the night. And sometimes the breathed-out sounds would become a bleating abundant with water. What was dangerous is that at no moment was there a mistake. Because it was the first time. And nothing could be repeated without making a mistake.

Then she cracked open her lips, breathing through them.

And then it really was from her mouth that the sweet confusion of the countryside was born. An instant however in which chastity was intensified and the pure voice would go off-key with love, now amidst the time of horses dragging wagons among the things.

In fact the breathing was already trembling, fecund, and there was already a threat in the burning heart of each vibration; the girl was sleeping with superhuman effort. Her breathing was already splitting on the first objects ... which were of an extrinsic beauty!

Could this be a new way of seeing things? of an extrinsic beauty! she was clapping sleepy hands. While the sounds were getting more and more in tune, since the first objects were already trying to give themselves: whatever existed was explaining itself as best it could, and the best it could was the trembling of a flower in the pitcher ... things arising and giving themselves in horror—and the best they could do was the serenity of a halted object.

Lucrécia Neves too was making an effort to give herself outward expression, without knowing whether to turn left or right. Suddenly she awoke.

The room was full of grace.

She was awake and difficult. From the shock of waking, she was unfurling in disarray around her own feet—feeling deathly ill. The nauseating music—she was still hearing it and couldn't believe it. Sitting on the bed in terror … She was awake and unaware—sleeping without interruption as if the earth were infinite.

Sleeping with monstrous patience. She was searching.

And now it was very late.

When she'd invented hearing the news, the girl had regressed to being dressed in long skirts and smoothing out plaits of hair on her forehead.

But now in the dream she could retreat until finding at last: that she was Greek.

"Like the Greek woman in the magazine," and she blushed, agitated. Dreaming of being Greek was the only way not to scandalize oneself; and to explain her secret in the form of a secret; to get to know herself in any other way would be the fear.

She was from before the Greeks had yet thought, it would be so dangerous to think.

A Greek in a city not yet erected, trying to designate each thing so that later, down through the centuries, they would have the meaning of their names.

And her life was erecting, with other patient lives, whatever would be later lost in the very form of things. She was pointing with her finger, the faceless Greek. And her destiny as a Greek then was as unconscious as now in São Geraldo. What had remained of what was so far away? what had remained of Greece? the persistence: since she was still pointing.

Then, with a sigh, she lay down in the garden to rest, repeating the ritual. And that's how she stayed.

While she'd dreamed, much time had already passed over her face. A more vivid feature had crumbled, spent, and the evidence of the expression. Her stone lips had cracked and the statue was resting in the darkness of the garden.

Only a disaster would fill with blood and modesty that deteriorated face that had achieved the cynicism of eternity. And that not even love would decipher. The empty sockets. She herself hardened into a single fragment—if they grabbed her by a leg they'd dislocate the whole body, now easily transportable.

And that's how they'd set her down. Upside down and feet together in the air.

Until, more and more gnawed at by time, she'd arise one day in order to continue her incomplete work in another city.

When all cities were erected with their names, they'd destroy themselves anew because that's the way it had always been. Upon the rubble horses would reappear announcing the rebirth of the old reality, their backs without riders. Because that's the way it had always been.

Until a few men would tie them to wagons, once again erecting a city that they wouldn't understand, once again building, with innocent skill, the things. And then once more they'd need a pointing finger to give them their old names. That's how it would be for the world was round.

But for now she could still rest.

In the cold darkness geraniums, artichokes, sunflowers, melons, hard zinnias, pineapples, roses were entwining. From the barge buried in the sand, only the prow was protruding. And, in the mutilated doorway, a rooster's head was keeping watch. Only with the coming of dawn would you see the broken column. And the flies. Around the chapiter, the feeble and shining germination of mosquitos.

But suddenly some thing was corrupted: new mosquitos were born — a sparrow flew! oh, it's still early, it's too early! yet in the darkness you could already glimpse the statue's eyes.

She'd have to get up — oh it's still early, rest is no nice! but you could already make out the broken mast coming out of the fog and already foresee where the garden wall would end. Around the statue's head the first bee was darting, coming out of the hard lips. And just beyond emerging from the mist, the rooster. The treasure. Oh it's still early, it's too early! yet the stone had been wounded by the chisel: the sun was rising.

And from the blackened mouth, in a quick sigh, the first halo of moisture was born.

Now, in the garden, neither darkness nor brightness — coolness. The breeze across the mutilated face amidst the cans.

Neither darkness nor brightness — dawn. There are three kingdoms in nature: animal, vegetable and mineral. And amidst the rusted cans the peacock displaying itself ... Neither darkness nor brightness — visibility.

When could more than that be done? The horse's head was eating the artichokes. And in the brighter sand the sleeping crocodile was revealed ... neither shadows nor light — visibility. Morning in the Museum. And the treasure. The treasure.

Lucrécia Neves trembled at last.

In her sleep she got up painfully, with her face ruined by the township. Until her rotted hands touched the railings of the park of São Geraldo. There she stood waiting, her passive face stuck to the bars. In a stable stirred the sleeping weight of hooves, the water rippled beyond the Gate. Beneath the changing tremblings of the brightness even the spots were already appearing on her face. Dawn—the lion was walking in his cage. Dawn.

Then Lucrécia flapped her wings.

With monotonous and regular flapping she was flying in the darkness above the city.

She was sleeping with monotonous, regular flapping.

In the middle of her sleep, in yet another stab of ferocity, Lucrécia Neves got up and paced the room on her four hooves, sniffing the darkness. What a room! that girl was stopping gentle on her hooves. What a room! she was moving her head from side to side with patience.

Finally she betook herself to sleep.

The color of the chamber was now reaching a sharp neutrality. Neither darkness nor brightness—visibility. The tall and early-rising buildings. Through the window the wind was chilling her hair and nothing else was fluttering in the room. The house was smelling entirely of old trees. Suddenly, bumped about in the cabriolet, with astonished seriousness, she fell asleep. The danger had passed.

She awoke with the military march of the scouts! drums ruffling among the baskets of fish.

She awoke late, the horses already lining up to go. The large vegetal ears of sleep were shrinking quickly to small and sensitive ears — the joy of the São Geraldo scouts was also condensed until becoming precise as painstaking bees.

Whatever had been damp, had been dried of rain. The girl found things already stuffed by the dry sun. Where was last night's storm? through the window she was seeing calm armies of centaurs advancing in the clouds, dragging their majestic posteriors. And on the side of the fields flocks of crows were cawing loudly announcing good weather …

In the street the procession — it was the trombone. The sounds were exciting the smell of fish, luminous spots were passing through the branches of the trees. The girl was looking at the scattered clothes, the room still enormous.

But amidst her incomprehension the military march was of a stunning reality. Telegram wires running across the open balcony and all of their sharp carrying-on had an immediacy — the day!

The girl still suspended in the room. At times spurring it on a bit, swaying on it. Looking from top to bottom, from the bed dangling from the floor; it had never been today until then.

The night's outsized wardrobe, now already shrunk, was simmering with clothes and hats. The brightness smelled of cut leaves: they were pruning the trees on Market Street, and the blades were raising dust as though from a construction site — São Geraldo was enormous, full of ladders leaning on the tree trunks, the furniture shaken by a constant violence that was: nine in the morning!: the clock tower started to strike, and the girl sneezed.

Having crossed the bumpy tunnel that was opening at last onto a room in a house — now she was peering out already awake, shrewd, Lucrécia—a foreigner protected only by a race of people all alike, scattered at their posts.

Two streets down three stone women were holding up the door of a modern building. The telegraph wires were trembling in dots and dashes ... With a leap Lucrécia Neves was at the balcony, her hands holding in check against her legs the nightgown that the wind was blowing.

At first she couldn't quite open her eyes because of the sun but soon there was the peaceful headquarters of the Commerce Association. The rooftops exposed. Crumbling mortar on the walls ... In the brightness a mason was shaking all over on his drill, calmly undermining the township through one of its stones. People were looking in the shop windows ... What had happened to the city of the night before?!

Like a bat the city was blind by day.

6 Sketch of the City

ON THAT DAY IT SO HAPPENED THAT LUCRÉCIA NEVES was in the kitchen at two in the afternoon.

Ana had gone out shopping, and silence was spreading in watchfulness throughout the house. It had often occurred before that the girl would do the dishes from lunch while her mother was shopping. It was a day like any other. And maybe it was precisely for this reason that, in a ripening, that afternoon was brightening particularly through the Venetian blinds of the windows. Where the light couldn't quite penetrate, there was restless darkness: the house was trembling all over.

What happened that afternoon went beyond Lucrécia Neves in a vibration of sound that would blend into the air and not be heard.

That's how she escaped finding out. The girl was lucky: she always escaped by just a second. It was true that, because of the difference of that second, someone else would suddenly understand. But it was also true that because of that same second someone else would be struck down: São Geraldo was full of resplendent people who quivered with joy in the ambulance of the Pedro II Psychiatric Hospital.

The main thing really was not to understand. Not even joy itself.

Water was pouring from the tap and she was running the soapy rag over the silverware. From the window you could see the yellow wall—yellow, the simple encounter with the color was saying. Scrubbing the teeth of the fork, Lucrécia was a small gear spinning quickly while the larger one was spinning slowly—the slow gear of brightness, and inside it a girl working like an ant. Being an ant in the light, was absorbing her completely and soon, like a true worker, she no longer knew who was washing and what was being washed—so great was her efficiency. She finally seemed to have surpassed the thousand possibilities that a person has, and to be only in this very day, with such simplicity that things were seen immediately. The sink. The pans. The open window. The order, and the peaceful, isolated position of each thing beneath her gaze: nothing was escaping her.

When she'd look for another bit of soap, it wouldn't occur to her not to find it: there it was, at her fingertips. Everything was at her fingertips.

Which was so important to a person to some extent stupid; Lucrécia who didn't possess the futilities of the imagination but just the narrow existence of whatever she was seeing. Ah! a bird was crying in the yard of the store.

Without makeup her face would lose those vices that at other times Lucrécia Neves would need to give herself a certain weight in this world. With her naked face, she too would go ahead if the little children called. All lit up, all of her measured by two o'clock. Ah! the bird in the yard was cutting across. Deep down, she thought she was a goddess.

Maybe it was in order to express her divinity that the girl

stopped tired, wiping the sweat from her brow with the arm that was holding the plate.

Running her gaze over the vast sunny township. There were the clipped-out things, and without shadows, made for a person to stand up straight while looking at them. With the plate in her hand, her tool, she would have liked to express maybe to her mother, for instance, the extent to which her daughter was … was …

A bit intrigued, she looked at those illuminated things around her, forcing herself now to give outward expression, with a real thought, to whatever was happening outside her.

Nothing was happening though: a creature was facing whatever it was seeing, taken by the quality of what it was seeing, with its eyes obfuscated by its own calm way of looking; the light in the kitchen was her way of seeing — things at two o'clock seem to be made, even in their depths, of the way their surfaces are seen. She really would have liked to tell Ana or Perseu something about this brightness.

But forsaken, strong, she was standing. Mulling over her inability to reason.

In that goddess consecrated by two o'clock, her thought, almost never utilized, had been perfected until transforming into merely one of her senses. Her most stripped-down thought was seeing, strolling, hearing. But her crude spirit, like a great bird, followed along without demanding explanations of itself.

And as for telling Perseu what was happening — it was all too simple, even stupid: she was just constructing whatever exists. What! she was seeing reality.

Besides which how could she tell Perseu or even manage to think, if all that were made of things of which if you were to demand proof … In order to sustain them, you just had to believe and not even address them—the whole kitchen was a sidelong vision. Whenever you turned to one side, the vision would once more be off to the side. That was how the girl was keeping up the illumination of two o'clock—now lifting her head at a sound, and now running through the house all the way to the balcony, summoned by the noise of many footsteps in the street.

She opened the doors to the balcony, saw seminarians walking down the sidewalk, lined up two by two and vague gestures, the flight of cassocks … Could they be happy? she wondered slyly. Sometimes Lucrécia Neves was terribly intelligent. She laughed. She looked at the store across the street.

And she looked at a third floor that the sun was fully brightening. One of the thousand bunkers of the stupid illuminated city.

But what pride in seeing the state of its perfect system of defense. Maybe one day armored cars would be posted on every corner. That bulwark. The glory of a person was to have a city.

And now, after crossing the shadowy hallways once again, the kitchen was opening into the parlor.

One more minute had already transformed it: now the previous way of seeing was no use. These changes seemed to leave Lucrécia extremely satisfied and the girl was looking at such lovely, such unswollen pans.

Oh, she'd never need more than all this, nothing extraordinary would ever tempt her, or her imaginings: in fact she liked whatever's there.

That was the question, "the thing that's there." You couldn't do anything but: go beyond it. And in order to go beyond it, having to consider it a supposition. But once in a while, it was no longer a hypothesis: it was the thing that's there. Lucrécia even used to tell anecdotes, but pretending they were true! and people would laugh much more, if they thought it was true—so frightening was the irremediable.

She'd believe in certain facts, not in others—she didn't believe that clouds were evaporated water: why should she? since the clouds were right there. Neither did she come close to liking anything poetic. What she really liked was people who talked about how things were, enumerating them somehow: that was what she'd always admired, she who in order to try to learn about a town square would make an effort not to fly over it, which would be so much easier. She liked to stay in the thing itself: the happy smile is happy, the big city is big, the pretty face is pretty—and thus whatever turned out to be clear was just her way of seeing.

Until, every once in a while, she'd see even more perfectly: the city is the city. Her crude spirit still lacked the ultimate refinement in order to be able to see just as if saying: city.

After she put away the dry dishes is when the true story of that afternoon began.

A story that could be seen in such different ways that the best way not to make a mistake would be just to enumerate the girl's steps and see her acting the way you'd just say: city.

The fact really is that Lucrécia Neves had leaned forward to beat dust off the broom in the backyard of the store. And on the windowsill of "The Golden Tie" was the orange on the plate.

It was a new way of seeing; limpid, indubitable. Lucrécia Neves peered at an orange on the plate.

Farther on the bin for bottles, the wooden crate, the decaying ledger, a dirty rag and the orange once again. The gaze was not descriptive, what was descriptive were the positions of the things.

No, whatever was in the yard was not an ornament. Some unknown thing had taken for an instant the form of this position. All this constituted the city's defense system.

Things seemed only to want: *to appear*—and nothing else. "I see"—was all you could say.

Going afterward to put away the dishrag, stopping now for a moment by Ana's bedroom, locked. Looking now through the keyhole. How big things seemed when seen through the aperture. They acquired volume, shadow and clarity: they *were appearing*. Through the keyhole the bedroom had a motionless, astonished wealth—which would disappear if you opened the door.

The city too should be spied upon through an embrasure. So whoever was spying, would defend himself, like the thing spied upon. Both out of reach. That's how Lucrécia was spying curious through the embrasure, almost squatting beside the keyhole. Within a maximum watchfulness she was unaware.

Standing up straight now with pain in her kidneys, going to the back balcony, and spreading out the damp towel.

And seeing the wall cut by the flat balcony with clean iron rods. Some thing was happening.

Looking, the girl seemed to be trying to keep the high wall with the balcony from existing, so that nothing could be done with them—just inexplicably see their existence. She breathed calmly, without overdoing it.

Everything she was seeing was becoming real. Looking now, without uneasiness, at the horizon sliced by smokestacks and rooftops.

The difficult thing is that appearance was reality. Her difficulty in seeing was as if she were painting. From every wall with a pipe something irreducible was being born—a wall with pipe. The pipes: how obstinate. When it was a heavy pipe it would be: wall with heavy pipe. There was no possible error—everything that existed was perfect—things only started to exist when perfect.

Opening now the storeroom, seeking a place to put the broom, looking. Some thing was happening over there: a rubber tube connected to a broken faucet was happening, an old coat hanging in the back, and electrical cord wrapping around an iron.

The materials of the city!

She was looking at the things that cannot be said. Certain arrangements of form would awaken that hollow attention in her: her merciless eyes looking, the thing letting itself be looked at mercilessly: a rubber tube connected to a broken faucet, the coat hanging behind it, the electrical cord wrapping around an iron. Seeing things is what things were. She was stomping her hoof, patient. Trying, as a way of looking at them, to be somehow stupid and solid and full of wonder—like the sun. Looking at them almost blind, obfuscated.

After years of stubbornness, whatever was crudely spiritual in her way of looking had been accentuated.

She was brutish, standing, a beast of burden in the sun. This was the deepest kind of meditation of which she was capable. Anyway all she had to do was think a little, and she'd become impermeable, the drowsy eye as an open way of seeing the things. Just the way of doing it, not the possessing; moving every once in a while the position of her legs.

I know what you're trying to do: you're trying to see the surface but your voice is hoarse, she thought so deep and unfamiliar that she seemed to have gone to an open field in order to think, quickly returning from there in order to go on.

You could think everything as long as you didn't know it. Though that was still risky. Oh, but she was careful.

Her caution would consist of having no idea what she was doing; she'd call her gaze "I'm putting away the broom"; and that precaution was enough. "Putting away the broom" was looking at the void of the little storeroom while, when a trolley passed, the entire house would shake with its trinkets, walls, clear windows and darkness.

Even error was a discovery. Erring would make her find the other face of objects and touch their dusty sides.

Spying. Because some thing wouldn't exist except under intense attention; looking with a severity and a hardness that were making her not seek the cause of things, but just the thing. Severe, brief, hoarse, real, immersed in dream.

Suddenly, as if ruffling her feathers, getting spooked: because they were untransformable things! rigid! unconsumable by paying attention! "The thing that's there" was the final impossibility.

And behind, the whitewash of the wall.

What a city. The invincible city was the ultimate reality. Beyond it there would be only dying, as a conquest.

But in the name of what king was she a spy? her patience was horrible. Her fear was that of surpassing whatever she was seeing. She was spying on the pipes, the coat and the electrical cords: they had the beauty of an airplane. Beautiful as eyeglasses—she blinked.

At the same time she was barely aware, sometimes scratching herself almost ironically—she had nothing to do until she found a husband. Leaning on one hip. Oh, she'd just briefly landed there. None of this had anything to do with her; she was looking around unburdened, a bit insolent.

And, if anyone thought the time had come to shout in order to scare her—he'd be the one frightened off when he saw her turn her head and peer calmly, slightly sarcastic, straight into the eyes of whoever wanted to frighten her. That's how Lucrécia Neves was, blinking.

And drawing away now with an indecipherable memory. Toc, toc, toc, she was walking erect. Toc, toc, toc,—that was her way of reducing all exterior things to a childish and mechanical noise with the heels of her horseshoes. The vision of the storeroom had had the same character as her taking a trolley one day! Or going to the dentist. Lovely as a motorcycle— she was clapping.

She then went to the back balcony, hung out the dishrag, looked at the yard—nobody could savor a deserted city like Lucrécia Neves, and without taking a crumb for herself. Without touching, without transforming: looking at the yard of the store, leaning her whole body forward. Among the ruins she saw the lizard running off and kicking up dust!

The most difficult part of the house was missing: the parlor, the garrison.

Where each clever thing would exist as if so that others wouldn't be seen? such was the great defense system. She began carefully, protecting herself with the thought that she was going in there to rest a little, mama, because I washed all the dishes, I'm exhausted.

The balcony was open. And in the middle the small table upon its legs. The chairs on guard. Oh, the infinite positions of the room, as if someone were lying on the floor and looking at the ceiling lamp sway ... you could get dizzy on the rim of a trinket. And they were always the same things: towers, calendars, streets, chairs—yet camouflaged, unrecognizable. Made for enemies.

The things were difficult because, if they explained themselves, they wouldn't go from incomprehensible to comprehensible, but from one nature to another. Just the gaze wouldn't alter them.

Beneath the wheels of a wagon, the mirror on the wall reflected itself in clarity and light. But gradually the wounded room stopped making sounds, while Lucrécia was calming down. Looking at her nails: that's what she was doing, those nails dulled by soap.

And, everything that had withdrawn with so much reserve upon her entrance, started breathing again full of wood, porcelain, worn varnish and shadow. In the mirror was floating the knowledge of the entire room.

The flower! the flowers were expressing themselves with petals, the curtain advancing to the middle of the room. Ana would remove the dust every day but couldn't dust the calm penumbra—and the room was growing old with the frozen trinkets.

Since Lucrécia Neves didn't understand them, she didn't know how to look at them: she was seeking one way, some other, and suddenly: there were the trinkets. Almost the word: the trinkets.

How to say that the trinkets were there? ah! she stared with brutality at those things made from the things themselves, falsely domesticable, hens that eat out of your hands but recognize you not—only borrowed things, one thing lent to another and another lent to another. Remaining on the shelves or staying indifferent on the floor and on the ceiling—impersonal and proud as a rooster. Since everything that had been created had at the same time been loosed.

Then Lucrécia, she herself independent, beheld them. So anonymously that the rules could be upended without a problem, and she'd be the thing seen by the objects.

It wasn't for nothing that she'd displayed herself so often on the hill in the pasture awaiting her turn.

Because now she seemed finally to have attained in herself the peak of those peaceful things beneath one's gaze. Moving her own stupidity forward with majesty to the highest point of the hill, her head dominating the township.

What you don't know how to think, you see! the maximum accuracy of imagination in this world was at least seeing: who'd ever thought up the daylight? at least Lucrécia was seeing and stomping her hoof.

Experiencing such exterior joy that it was already other people's joy that she was feeling, impersonal god for whom the clouds were a way for him not to be on earth and the mountains his way of being farther off.

The girl's joy was like this:

The flowers in the pitcher. One was red. It had a weak stem. One was pink. The table. It was small. On the dusty floor its legs touching down. A flower was sagging under the weight of the flower's corolla. The rectangular window. Empty on the wall. The trinket holding out the flute. The larger flower was pale, with a thick corolla.

Lucrécia might not have been reaching whatever was around her, and was just taking a step when faced with the fact of the room—but this is the place where the things are. The corner of the dark room. The wall leaning back. The roof made of light wooden planks, dirty. The bookcase. The door. The floor. The angle. The clock. Flower, pitcher, ceiling, floor, blinds. And, hurled from afar, a confused object that in front of her face took shape clear and enlarged: the perfect chair.

Lucrécia Neves looked at it and made with her face, imperceptibly, the expression of the chair.

Her thought just then was after all very innocent and visible: a thought with four legs, a seat and a back. With this reflection she seemed to have grasped to the very end the perfection of things.

If she hadn't been able to pierce the city's walls, at least she was now part of those walls, in whitewash, stone, and wood.

Then, possessing the gesture learned on the rainy night, with her left hand outstretched and her foot advancing—she performed it delicate, rigid. Pointing with grace and precision.

Oh, just one of those pirouettes of a girl ready to marry. They're so happy. Sometimes they even do somersaults right in front of other people, and burst out laughing afterward.

But this time Lucrécia learned even less than the cashier: finishing up cleaning her nails, she rubbed them on the leather of the seat, checked the shine that the soap had dulled, yawned and left.

7 The Alliance with the Outsider

BUT IN THE MORNING, AT BREAKFAST, EVERYTHING was yellow and when a daughter was drinking coffee and the steam was coming out of the cup, yellow flowers had spread over the table, and a mother seated at the head of the table was the lady of this house: Ana reigned.

The floral wallpaper how it would start the day old. When Ana was sitting, her badly braided hair would get tangled in the wallpaper with pink daisies, green on the stems, purple at their tips—but everything was auburn. In the dewy night air there had grown throughout the rooms bushy trees that were shaking in a wet park fragrance—the steam was coming from the coffeepot blackening the house in a dream.

Ana was grabbing the cookie crumbs around the cup and shoving them greedily into her mouth, clumsily as in a hospital. You couldn't tell that, by concentrating on small acts, she was enjoying the morning in the house, applying herself with nearsightedness to things, handling the cookie, blowing her nose, washing herself with care; her life would sometimes have this delicateness.

Meanwhile, outside, the noises of the street were growing more excited, the smell of the stable stirring at the first winds, and the sounds intertwining the way walls are constructed: the city was imperceptibly rebuilding itself.

But Lucrécia was hardly helping the widow's morning joy. The short cloak, taking her back to the time when she was growing up, the girl was relaxing with her elbows leaning on the table, disheveled, big.

And if they spoke, in every thought a delusion and a dream were almost palpable, from the coffeepot blackened vapors were emerging; but they were the mother and the daughter, offering themselves to one another as hands are offered to one another; and, though they thought themselves to be exceptionally sharp, they'd never tried to prove it.

"You're not going out today, are you, Lucrécia."

"Maybe, maybe not."

"You're getting bored, why not keep busy?"

"If it were just once and that was it," the girl answered suddenly intimate, her strength slipping away—"but to keep busy every day!"

She needs to get married, Ana thought, and it was the truth.

"You need to calm down," Ana said voluptuous from having her to herself for a whole morning, "you were always like this, for as long as I can remember, if I'd kept a diary you'd see, my dear girl."

A diary, she was saying like someone who kept up with what was going on in the world ... Lucrécia looked at her with astonishment.

But before long she was lowering her eyes to the coffee cup thinking about what Ana hadn't said, maybe guessing her plans for marriage.

The subject, brought on by the girl's understanding, then became easy to broach.

"You've gone out with lots of people, Mateus is the only one you haven't seen, isn't that right, my dear girl ... it's true he's much older ..."

"That's not why ... to the contrary ... Ah, Mateus is from another milieu, mama! he comes from another city, he's got culture, knows what's going on, reads the paper, knows other people ..."

"... does good business," Ana said weakly.

"True," Lucrécia granted, "true ..."

"And since I'm not going to live my whole life ..."

What whole life was she referring to if not her own? and how could she not live her own whole life even if she were to die at any moment? Lucrécia Neves was reflecting.

"If you married him you'd have lots of things, hats, jewels, live well, get out of this hole ... have a nicely furnished house, ..." Ana continued horrified by the path she'd finally taken, her hand rising to her neck.

Lucrécia Neves looked at her with fright, feigned, as if too innocent to grasp—soon laughing disagreeably, while her desire would be to finally turn her back on São Geraldo. Without noticing she was already sketching the movement of freedom, when she met Ana's gaze.

Her mother's simplicity embarrassed her—if she married Mateus what would she do with Ana, so inexperienced and wistful, and so delicate, in the luxurious milieu they'd inhabit? her mother would be "afraid."

"You didn't eat anything ..." Ana was saying offended while looking at the intact cookie.

Instead of answering, Lucrécia had stood and was already climbing the three cement steps, crossing the hallway and penetrating the living room lowering her head in order to pass beneath the doorway, though it was taller than she was: imitating, in obscure compensation, the habit of her dead, tall father.

She'd hardly sat down with her embroidery in her hands, when the door was opening and half of Ana's face appeared, smiling confusedly like the man you see in the moon …

"… you didn't even drink your milk …"

"I did already," she lied. Ana knew it, but would never get near her lies.

"Fine," she answered—she was hesitating at the door hoping Lucrécia would want her.

But Lucrécia smiled drawing things to a close, and Ana repeated: fine, my girl, closing the door with a sigh.

The poor woman hated São Geraldo and they would have already moved if, she'd say with reproach, Lucrécia weren't such a patriot. Even the house carried a whiff of the city, and both of them smelled it, Lucrécia rejoicing, Ana wanting to talk all day long in order to escape.

Because once or twice they'd both been deeply moved by some misfortune that didn't concern them—which would spark enormous interest in Ana, as long as it hadn't happened in São Geraldo—now the mother would come always with newspaper in hand, looking her daughter straight in the eye: a child in F …, eighteen months old, had swallowed a white bean and choked. Poor child, she was sighing with watchfulness, at least it won't suffer anymore. Lucrécia would stir afflicted.

And now again the door was opening, interrupting her embroidery. Ana said ironically: Perseu again …

He showed up immediately as if he'd been listening at the door.

He came in looking around with indiscretion; his beautiful

eyes were moving but his mouth was shut as if he were holding something back for later. It was true that in the morning he was always lovely and clever. But Lucrécia, quite distrustful, noticed that this time it was because he'd decided to change his approach. In what way, she didn't know; neither did Perseu for that matter.

"Good morning," said the young man only when the door closed, as if Ana shouldn't hear this secret.

Nobody answered him. Lucrécia Neves was looking at him letting him know, that if he changed his approach, he'd be alone. Perseu Maria didn't seem bothered, pulled out a chair and sat straight up in front of her—transforming the peaceful room into a knot.

Then, with insulting calm, he looked at everything a bit, even stared at Lucrécia's legs, which filled her with rage—he however feigned disinterest and quickly examined the girl's ears. They were emerging from her dark hair as donkey ears and seemed to hear from afar with insolence.

But not a single word was spoken. She wasn't even looking at him. Perseu, without getting distracted, kept examining his surroundings, resting his gaze on one trinket or another as if all of a sudden surprised by them and at the same time knowing how to deal with them—he had an aptitude for mechanical things and wanted to apply his heavy hands to everything. Finally he noticed that Lucrécia was observing him and he was bothered:

"They're yours ..." he asked pointing with his face.

"They belong to the room."

He looked at her with surprise and joy:

"Nonsense! things belong to people!"

"They belong to the room," Lucrécia Neves grumbled.

"And the room, sweetheart?"

"It belongs to the house, the house belongs to São Geraldo, don't annoy me."

"Ah. And São Geraldo?"

"It ... It belongs to São Geraldo, leave me alone."

"Fine, fine! no need to yell."

So it was true: he'd changed his approach.

"They belong to the room, I already told you," she repeated firm but more cautious.

Again he seemed to keep his cool and only made himself more comfortable in the chair.

"Yesterday we went for a walk."

"Who's we," doubted the girl.

The young man's eyes shone with intelligent laughter:

"Who? come on now! the walk went for a walk!"

How quickly he'd understood! she hurried to correct him:

"What I said was a joke, you know, sometimes I even pretend that the trinkets belong to São Geraldo, imagine that. But they belong to people, naturally, you're so silly"—and since it was hard for her to lie so much, she added laughing—"but no one knows to whom, buddy ..."

"I know," said Perseu just to say something.

Seeing however the gaze of curiosity that was thrown toward him, he rose like a demon in a burst of joy, leaned against the wall getting ready to flee if necessary:

"Well I know, *I* know!"

"But you're just ridiculous!"

Though really humiliated by the insult, the young man didn't budge from his position at the wall, his arms apart in the form of a cross—he just cowered a bit and turned his head, wounded. "*I* know," he repeated this time in anger.

"Whose are they?" she finally asked with effort.

They remained for a moment in silence, staring at each other.

"God's, for example, …" Perseu said, he too disappointed, drawing in his arms and shrinking.

But she was now the one who seemed ready to advance, bristling.

"They're not even God's, they belong to themselves, idiot!"

"Fine, fine!" the fellow was spooked.

They remained in careful silence. Without making a sound, he returned to the chair avoiding insulting her with a glance.

At last, when he imagined everything must have calmed down, he lifted, cautious, his eyes.

With surprise he saw that Lucrécia Neves had not only composed herself but was seated imperiously.

Feeling observed, the girl imagined this would be the time to quash the young man's plans to make changes, if he wasn't already defeated. Entirely calm and indifferent, she started peering at her own hand as if it didn't belong to her, turning it around and around and moving her fingers as if waving or running them like rats over the arm of the chair: showing Perseu her juggling ability. When at last she got from him the old look that said terrified: you're extraordinary!, she forsook herself satiated.

But now it was he who wouldn't forsake her.

He was staring at her in a deceptive way, almost about to jump on top of her.

Lucrécia Neves had irritated him. He could marry her one day and transform her, the way a man can give a woman a beating; but he still had the courtesy to leave the job to someone else.

Which didn't keep him from being so annoyed that he might, in a grand and single swipe, break those dirty trinkets!

Just then the young man seemed to understand that she liked them a lot, and he detested her and detested them, for after all! he was a man! he couldn't stand courtesies any longer, and would sweep away in a single gesture the smart little ladies of São Geraldo, their trinkets, their whims—and be alone.

This was the fellow's cruel desire, looking at her with ferocity. Lucrécia, under threat, was growing larger in defense, both of them staring at each other in rage, but the truth sneakily transforming itself: he with his wrinkled brow, she already frightened, he masculine, she feminine, she light, he heavy, she bad and he good. Realizing before he did the situation they were in, the girl looked at him in defiance. Perseu recoiled.

Both stared at each other disappointed and alert.

Oh, he really wanted her, Perseu felt; suddenly she was necessary to him just as the girl seemed to need furniture, trinkets; was he needing her in order for her to make some thing concrete with her presence? in a fleeting, almost negative, movement, that's how he understood her for an instant.

Meanwhile Lucrécia was reigning looking at her fingernails. One day he'd touched her shoulders in order to show her some thing and felt the bones of that person who thought herself a queen …

He quickly started to tell her about the plans he'd made for an outing, the reason after all for his morning visit:

"We'll take the trolley at the market, get off at the second plaza, from there we'll take the road to …"

Soon, interested, she was following the plan.

And soon, both of them distracted, they once again seemed

to think about the same thing, about the love that had failed a few minutes ago — and she'd never forgive.

And he knew he'd done what he had to in order to continue down his slow path that was calling him more than a woman. But he was ashamed of hitting the mark.

They fell quiet at the same time. The girl was examining her fingernails, the fellow his shoes.

"This morning I was sleeping" — she said suddenly like a child — "when some thing woke me, but then I fell back asleep, and dreamed that someone was giving each person their lost sleep, in order for us to get it back, you know? then they asked me if for me it was a thousand or two thousand years of sleep, so I said two thousand, then they closed my eyes again and so I …"

"But who?" interrupted Perseu Maria shifting in his chair.

"Who what?" she asked annoyed. "Didn't I say it was 'some thing'? — well then" — she kept smiling once again in gluttony and haste — "I was closing my eyes and going back, back, until this was I sleeping, I mean" — and she grew irritated for having to explain even without his asking — "this was I being asleep." — She stopped disappointed. — "And you?" she asked after the pause in a rivalry that curiosity was winning.

"Nothing, I didn't dream anything!" he answered ardently, so bothered he was by Lucrécia Neves's dreams.

Disillusioned, she stared at him trying to read into those sweet eyes, into that timid and dark-skinned figure in which, whatever ugliness it had, was beauty on Market Street. She might never find such a beautiful man, she thought with regret lowering her eyes to hide a certain greed:

"If my mother died I'd go live with you."

"What!"

The young girl descended from her own absorbed gaze and managed to look straight at him in the midst of imagining:

"We're not going to get married, but we're like fiancés."

And that's how it was. He was astonished with wonder: "it's true," he mumbled looking at the ceiling, his mouth looking as if about to whistle.

"What do you think, should I leave?" he finally asked, miserable.

"Yes, go," she said with much courtesy.

Since he wasn't getting up Lucrécia Neves added with kindness:

"Mama cut her finger you know with what?"

"With what ..." he asked with distrust.

"With paper ... It was fine paper. It sliced her so that her flesh didn't even open up. It just scratched her and blood came out."

"That's a lie," he said shrewdly.

"You always think anything you don't believe is a lie," the girl answered with haughtiness. "She even put disinfectant on it. Paper can cut, too, buddy, go ask your dad ..."

"... I'm leaving," he retorted upset extending his hand. She laughed:

"People like us don't need to shake hands!" and she was trying to muffle her laughter because Perseu had blushed and withdrawn his hand, but she couldn't. And as she was laughing while showing her separated teeth, he left almost at a run in horror, bumping into the shelf.

Alone, so suddenly, the girl hardly had time to finish laughing.

The sun, nearing noon, was beaming into the mirror. From the balcony was coming a smell of train, of trees and of coal—the smell of invaded countryside that São Geraldo had; she herself drew back lazily, travelling jolted in the room. And finally, beneath the noise of wheels, her senses dulled until she dozed off.

Had her unfettered spirit joined the wind through the open window? and growing more and more distinct, she was an object of the room: her feet were resting on the floor, her body revealing itself in its sex and shape. Everything that had been supernatural—her voice, her gaze, her way of being—had ended; what was still left is what was making the house shiver. This would have been the moment for someone to look at her, and see her. And for the person's eyes to be wounded by the hard shine of the little ring on her finger, whose stone was gathering within itself the power of the room.

The door opened and her mother woke her:

"You called me …"

Lucrécia Neves opened her eyes, peered out without understanding. Much time had passed.

"Are you all right?" worried Ana. "Your face is so flushed …"

"I don't know … I'm hungry," she said loudly, scratching herself with difficulty.

"Hungry," thought the surprised mother.

She'd never heard this daughterly voice. Yes, Ana said pulling herself back together with difficulty into new maternity, she's hungry, she repeated, foolish, for others to hear and judge, and to know that her daughter had said, in her most childish and selfish voice, that she was hungry. Ah, girl, your health is back, she said hesitantly, your health is back, she repeated as she left to get the milk, dumbfounded, a bit bitter.

Lucrécia Neves was smiling in mystery and stupidity. She was hungry, yes, and was scratching her face with her nails; she really looked fat; in fact she'd reached an age.

From now on she might not have anything else to lose. Now it would be too late even to die.

Smiling, pretty, looking at her right hand where she soon wanted to see an engagement ring. More than a ring of engagement, of alliance.

8 The Betrayal

A MONTH AFTER SELLING OUT SÃO GERALDO, SHE
went with Mateus's friend to deal with the paperwork for her
marriage.

The friend said:

"Wait on that corner while I go into the notary's office."

The girl then answered:

"Of course, sir."

And on the corner she stayed, clasping her purse. She was
calm though suspicious.

With careful consideration she kept looking from side to
side, calculating and measuring this new city she'd bought.

But she wasn't some sacrificed innocent. Lucrécia Neves
wanted to be rich, own things and move up in the world.

Like the ambitious girls of São Geraldo, hoping that their
wedding day would free them from the township—that's how
she was, serious, dressed in pink. New shoes and hat. To some
degree attractive. To some degree enigmatic. Smoothing out
a crumpled crease in her skirt, tapping a bit of dust from her
sleeve. Occasionally giving a polite sigh.

But, perhaps led astray by the wind, perhaps because she was standing on a street corner—soon she was cracking open lips that the air was drying, and smiling. Modest in her crime, guiltless. Sometimes she'd clutch her purse, sighing enraptured.

And when the lawyer turned up again so busy, she looked at him from afar almost foolish, set loose on these streets that were not her own, with a man who was speaking and leading—a lawyer! The first element of Mateus's that she really was getting to know.

And the first technical manifestation of this new city where she was going to live. The dust was creeping over the sidewalks and the light wrinkling her face.

Lucrécia was all decked out. Ana had helped her get dressed, weeping—while she herself was still keeping back a feeling with which to just start off the wedding, a feeling she didn't know how to initiate and it was already almost time …

"… right this way," the lawyer was informing her looking at her quickly, once again surprised at the backwoods bride that Mateus, always unpredictable, had discovered—then Lucrécia Neves replied with a grave smile.

It's destiny, she was whispering to herself while following him as fast as she could in that kind of shoe, clasping the hat that the wind wanted to whisk off—it's destiny, she was saying pleased to be subjugated. Happy though anxious because she found the lack of danger odd.

On the sidewalks full of people nobody was looking at her, whose pink dress would nonetheless be charming in São Geraldo.

She also wanted to waste no time and look at the new city right away—this, yes! a true metropolis—that would be the outsider's prize—every man seemed to promise a woman a bigger city.

She was seeking a way all her own to look and that's how, through the triangle formed by the arm that was keeping her hat on her head, she saw a man running to catch the trolley …

In fact the new things were the ones looking at her and she was passing between them running after the lawyer. Once outside the township, her type of beauty had disappeared, and her importance had diminished. Anyway she didn't have time to think because the lawyer was inviting her for a coffee. She then became solemn, accepted with a nod, reproaching herself for getting distracted at times like this. She was pleased to be starting off right away the ritual of the new life, with forethought she sat on her pleated skirt. Even cakes came to the table … She ate one, with her pinky raised and the other hand catching crumbs. How frightened Ana would be! Both cake and mouth dry. And inside the cup the coffee was trembling at the passing of vehicles.

Some thing without interest to anyone was happening, surely "real life." Meanwhile in this "real life" Lucrécia Neves had started by being anonymous. Which in the end wasn't so bad; at least it was much broader. The dog entered the café, headed straight for the girl, touching her high heels.

"Go, go," she said firm and smiling, "go, go."

He didn't. And, miserable, he was sniffing her patent leather shoes with sadness, thoroughness and need. Amongst all those people he'd recognized her—"go!" she exclaimed so tragic and exhausted that the lawyer asked:

"He's bothering you that much?"

"Yes, he is," she answered with a broken voice, smiling …

He said:

"Out!," shooing him with his hand.

The dog immediately left in no hurry.

She laughed surprised.

"He left, sir ..."

The lawyer however was no longer looking at her, once again occupied with his stack of papers. Then Lucrécia Neves took back her smile. She coughed a little in a sign indecipherable in its subtlety. She was ceremonious and happy on the threshold of the big city. A fire-truck siren was going by announcing her.

9   The Exposed Treasure

THERE WASN'T SO MUCH AS A GESTURE THAT COULD express the new reality.

And, amidst this wealth, was Lucrécia Correia disheveled in a "robe de chambre," unable to rule over the treasure, scarcely guessing how far the magnificent basement extended. She'd now lost certain cares regarding herself, intensely happy, dragging along, peeking out, trying to inventory the new world that Mateus had unleashed with the diamond on his middle finger.

She finally seemed not to have time for anything, the way people don't.

The hotel, where Mateus and Lucrécia had set themselves up, offered an already old-fashioned comfort. None of the guests however would trade it for something more modern. Even the tattered drawing rooms reminded them of the time of poverty and abundance in the family—and above all "the other city" from which they'd all come.

In the "salon" decorated with palms the friezes on the walls were already revealing the rotten wood behind them, and the flies in the dining room brought the big city back to the age when there were flies. Though, in a few days, the recently married woman felt it had been years since she'd seen a cow or a horse.

It was in this setting, favorable to a ripening and a decomposition, that Mateus regally set up Lucrécia Neves. Right after the first lunch she came to understand her husband's ring.

"I hope you'll be happy here," he said to her, and he had the modest appearance of having shown part of his character.

To Lucrécia, the remains of a poorly buried ostentation were as fascinating as the continuous noise of that city.

For if in São Geraldo the engines were invisible, here they'd emerged, and you couldn't tell what was an engine and what was already a thing. Lucrécia came to consider herself the most inexperienced member of the city, and would let herself be led by her husband in visits to "places," with the hope of soon understanding the taxis crossing amidst cries of newspaper boys and those women with nice shoes jumping over the mud.

Because this city, in contrast to São Geraldo, seemed to be displaying itself all the time and the people were displaying themselves all the time.

Mateus Correia took her to the Museum, to the Zoo, to the National Aquarium. That was how he kept showing her what he was made of: showing her things he'd seen; patient, waiting for that woman to become just like him.

She understood everything attentively, as if being taught where to hang her dresses, where the bathroom was and where to turn on the light.

At the Museum, arm in arm—they'd seen old machines in their lengthy evolution until becoming that essential thing: modern. She was understanding everything, admiring her husband.

But at the National Aquarium, as much as she tried she couldn't figure out what "thing of his" Mateus had seen. And tired of rummaging through her spouse's soul—which seemed to have spread all over the city, plunging into this end only to turn up different and unmistakable at the other—already tired and finally taking a break, she looked on her own: the fish.

Several times Mateus tried to pull her away. But she, in a sign of future cruelty, stood firm. With a touch of rage she was seeing in the aquarium inserted into the wall the surface of the water—from bottom to top. From bottom to top—seeing fish almost touching the surface and returning with a gentle swoosh of the tail, and again advancing smoothly, trying with insomniac patience to go beyond the line of water.

The only place where they could live was a prison to them. That's what she saw, stubborn, comparing the water of the fish to São Geraldo—and giving the first nudge with her elbow to Mateus who kept wanting to leave.

Even in his city, Mateus Correia was still an outsider, a man who from every place would take whatever benefited him. He was constantly rushing around on the street but always calm and elegant. His flanks were frigid, and so were his legs and neck—the result perhaps of that muteness with which he'd lock himself in for his hour-long bath. He'd come out cold, his gray hair fragrant. His flat nails turning livid would dig into his big hand: in the pocket of his jacket a perfumed kerchief. The air of a lawyer or engineer—such was his air of mystery. She took no interest in her husband's business—but how he dressed up!

A continuous training. He was masculine and servile. Servile without humiliation like a gladiator who hired himself out. And she, being a woman, would serve him. She'd wipe his sweat, smooth his muscles. It demeaned her to live by dint of Mateus's comings and goings and his exercises, spreading out shirts that the dust of the city would immediately soil, or feeding him meats and wines. But she couldn't help being fascinated by that meticulous order, which seemed long since to have surpassed any justification, except to waste the months preparing him for combat.

Awaiting the day someone would at last crush her colossus—and, with horror, she'd be free. Whenever he'd return to the hotel, his wife would be surprised to see him still on the loose. There everyone seemed to live illicitly anyway, from extraordinary occupations. Mateus Correia for example was: an intermediary.

This function made him enigmatic and satisfied: he'd eat little in the morning, kiss her, his mouth through the coffee smelling of toothpaste and morning nausea. He wore rings on his fingers like a slave.

And after helping him get ready, she'd stay seated at the table, watching him move around. Everything was Mateus Correia now. Mateus's baths. Mateus's brushes. Mateus's fingernail scissors. Never had a more secretly exterior life been seen than his: she was stunned while watching him. She wouldn't even have to get to know him better.

And he was very witty too. "Sometimes I die laughing, mama," she'd write in her free time. Ana had moved to her sister's farm.

Lucrécia herself had been caught up by some gear of the perfect system. If she'd thought that by allying herself with an outsider, she'd shake off São Geraldo forever and tumble into fantasy? she'd been mistaken.

She'd tumbled in fact into another city—what! into another reality—the only reason it was more advanced was because it was a big metropolis where things had already been so mixed up that the inhabitants, either lived in an order superior to them, or were trapped in some gear. She herself had been caught by one of the gears of the perfect system.

Perhaps badly caught, with her head upside-down and one leg sticking out.

But from her position, maybe even a privileged one, she could still watch quite well. Standing, at the door of the hotel. Seeing the thousands of hired gladiators crossing back and forth. And while those statues were passing by—the rats, real rats, with no time to lose, were gnawing at whatever they could, taking advantage of the situation, shaking with laughter. What did you do this summer? they were asking suffocating with laughter, did you go dancing? In good conscience you couldn't say that the gladiators had gone dancing. To the contrary, they were extraordinarily methodical.

Already with a desire for a superior order, Lucrécia hoped to go two or three more times to the theater, waiting for the moment she'd reach a hard-to-count number, like seven or nine, and could add this sentence: "I used to go to the theater all the time."

Sitting with the audience, while the "ballet" was continuing on stage; the darkness was being cooled by fans. She had joined a people and, being part of that nameless crowd, was feeling both famous and unknown. Beyond the box, beyond the darkness, she could make out a ballroom—another ballroom—another ballroom—fleeing. In the hallways, the tips of toes arriving late, hands drawing back curtains, and breathless the people adding themselves to the darkness ... she herself excited by the fans, perspiring in her first married lady's black dress—"I got married in the summer," as it should be.

Onstage legs and feet were dancing without Lucrécia Neves Correia's quite understanding. From the intimate incomprehension of Market Street, she'd passed to public incomprehension. She tried her best to pick up other people's facial expressions and those terms with which Mateus's world would display knowledge of the finer points, the professional part of things. She was always tapping imaginary specks of dust from her dress and this precious gesture betrayed great insights. But, despite her efforts, she managed to watch the "ballet" merely fascinated. Not to mention that from afar it was impossible to make anything out except with binoculars. Over her neckline her husband's binoculars were blinding her face.

Telling herself with hitherto unknown care: you have to forget the dancer.

Because the just-married woman was trembling possessed by love for the dancer. Don't leave me, she was saying fanning herself ceremoniously. Mateus Correia was offering her bonbons—he bought her everything, and Lucrécia was already starting to get irritated with this man who had taken her because it gave him pleasure to have a young and flighty woman—the dancer, in elastic and languid movement, filled her with surprise, ripped open a vein of blood in her mouth: she mixed it into the sweetness of the bonbon, cleaning her teeth with her fingernail.

Her lack of sensuality was a heartily repugnant sensuality, her mouth full of blood, loving the dancer. Above all what was he giving himself to? she was remembering—in him she was seeing herself again on a rainy night, trying to point things out—as he himself was horrifyingly attempting.

He was the dancer of that city.

But if she could read Perseu's face, Ana's, Felipe's, and even Dr. Lucas's—she couldn't read the dancer's, it was a face that was too clear.

What was he giving himself to? she felt forewarned. Though she still understood the dancer's performance better than the city's other demonstrations. If he was awakening the old commitment in her, she was now out of time, her skirts caught by some gear of the perfect system. At the same time nobody would take her away from there, she had the right to be in a box: this was her time. The extraordinary guarantee.

Soon intermission was lighting up the whole theater, the dancer disappearing in a leap, the whole city applauding. Then she was getting up with Mateus, safeguarded, dragging her hips like a peacock. The breathing of the people was filling the ballrooms with heat, each thing proliferated by the mirrors in the middle of the night. In an advanced city each bit of news was spread by radio, each gesture multiplied by mirrors—care was taken to make something of the movements achieved.

All this, however, was at the beginning of the marriage.

Because later she learned to say: I really liked it, the show was good, I had such a nice time. The superior order. It was so well danced, she learned to say moving eyebrows, and freed herself forever from so many insurmountable realities. This is the most beautiful square I've ever seen, she'd say, and then could cross with security the most beautiful square she'd ever seen.

That's how it was. What a quick hunt. She'd go out to shop, walking in the shade looking at the dentists' signs, the bolts of cloth on display; up to the store was close, past it was "far": she was making calculations in the new landscape, comparing it with São Geraldo's.

Oh, you couldn't even compare them. A bit further they were repaving a street, and the perfected tools were heating up in the sun. In a few days the paving wouldn't be so up-to-date. And even more perfected instruments would come along to work on it. Several passersby were looking at the machines. Lucrécia Neves Correia too. The machines.

If a person didn't understand them, he was entirely out of it, almost absent from this world. But if he did understand them? If he did he was entirely inside, lost. The best approach would still be to leave, pretending not to have seen them—that's what Lucrécia did, resuming her shopping.

Back again, at the entrance into the dining room on Mateus Correia's arm, having to fake happiness despite being so happy: bananas for dessert. What a terrible noon in the city: irons simmering: I married in the summer! everyone eating every dish on the menu. It was allowed, the crisis still hadn't broken out. Then her husband was leaving, his mustache, the newspaper. No one to knock on the door and deliver a message: I don't mingle with people at the hotel, she thought all haughty in the room with the blinds closed where she was trying to sleep because Mateus wanted her to fatten up even more, even more, even more.

Oh, she couldn't even sum up Mateus, sitting beside him in the ice cream parlor.

He was wearing a wide-brimmed hat. And he'd let the nail of his pinky finger grow longer than the others. With a wide brim and a long nail—Mateus? No, he wasn't ruthless. But things had arranged themselves in such a way that it seemed to her urgent to get on his good side and make him pity her. How she'd flatter him! a sycophant, that's what she was. Also because she wanted more presents.

And when there was a party?

Suddenly there'd be a party, invitations arranged without much of a right, they seemed to manage everything through prohibited means, everyone fending for themselves as best they could—the world was turning, she was choosing all sweaty the fabrics, Mateus giving advice, she, finally uncovering her arms, the beginning of her breasts. She entered the ballroom.

Arm resting on her husband's, skirt dragging in the dust, lights, the women more beautiful than she, whose back was bare, and her placid arms also bare—finally she'd gained weight. And he! with a mustache, servile, dominating. It was at that moment that he was entirely unknown to her, within this already familiar lack of knowledge in which both understood each other. He was walking off to greet someone, Mateus! her mute voice crossing the ballroom, crossing the windows open to the moonlight, what did she care about the moonlight!—her gaze running amidst the noises of the skirts, what did she care about the dry moonlight, Mateus! because he was the blind guide but the guide—Mateus! who with his back to her was examining from head to foot another woman who wasn't even naked.

Not to mention the mirror that was distorting him on his mustache. And revealing a new expression, conceited and extremely smooth … So charming that even she smiled. Mateus was fat and handsome. And dangerous? like an acrobat. He seemed to take care never to mix himself up with himself. He was the result, in the mirror, of the display of someone else. She, who had always wanted the true things, wood, iron, house, trinket. Sometimes people would say: I saw you with your father, ma'am; she'd rejoice offended.

And that's how her husband asked her to dance, with a politeness that was making him even more unknown. And the great dancer of São Geraldo stumbling with her first steps ... Stepping on his feet. Where was her importance? and the living room? and amidst all this she was so happy that she was suffocating. "I achieved the Ideal of my life," she wrote to Ana.

"Have you ever seen so much food," Mateus said as proud as if the party were his, that was how each one seized whatever he could, "you can tell it's got something to do with the Government."

"That's true!" she retorted full of joy, amazing herself that Lucrécia from São Geraldo had climbed so high that she was mingling with people who ran a city, what! a country ...

They were going back to the hotel by car—he sure knew how to spend money! she was fanning herself radiant. But he should let her sleep.

"I'm tired," she informed him with a wife's cunning.

And if the moonlight was starting up again with its dead silence, the universal surroundings were avoiding the true night; the intimate mode was reducing itself to the impersonal. Profoundly happy.

Only an old commitment was no longer being fulfilled. She could still see, and was seeing. She'd fallen however from the surface of things to the inside.

Sometimes it would rain, was calm, she'd say:

"Today's Thursday, Mateus"—and everything was brought up-to-date.

He was incapable of saying an ugly word, and when in rage he'd let slip the beginning of one, she'd lean back in the chair laughing with her head lowered, laughing a lot—and her husband would look at her with surprise, flattered—angry and flattered:

"I didn't even say anything," he'd say laughing with modesty, she helping him to be a type, "I didn't even say anything!" he'd exclaim, and his wife would laugh beneath the catastrophe.

Besides flattering him, the rest was scrutinizing him uselessly. Bewildered. Those creatures didn't feel the slightest need to explain themselves—such was their mystery. With the clean nails of a man who knows about things and who drinks without getting drunk. And really very good to her:

"If you need anything, tell me, my girl."

Lucrécia Neves would seize the opportunity:

"Speaking of which, well then I've been needing a dress with frills on the sleeves and skirt."

He wouldn't say no, ah, never: he'd give her everything. "I have everything I dream of," she'd write her mother immediately, ready to jot down one more piece of information. Finally she imagined that he must surely have a mistress, since he was so masculine and mysterious! She started searching his pockets.

Until opening his desk drawer she found the envelope. She opened it with the help of steam and found inside the x-ray of two teeth.

Yes! but all this was happier, the days were passing, months and months were passing, hours being lost—and behind it all that established law, the newspapers being published, a generation feeling secure—and so often it had been her turn to be the guilty one, both would be running late or missing the trolley, ah, and looking for and not finding a street? I got lost, Mateus dear, I don't know the city, and being late, the hesitations, how often the hesitations like changes of light, and there was no need to force the union of one segment to another, it was enough to go to sleep in order to wake up the next day, sometimes later, sometimes earlier.

The main thing was not to leave your place out of impatience. To have a lot of perseverance indeed. And you'd finally reach, like now, a certain point. Brought by taxis, by waking up next day quite a bit earlier, by indeterminately getting Mateus ready: all this had brought her to the point of eating little sour oranges, closing her eyes while the man was asking:

"My girl, don't you think so."

"Yes, yes," she'd say restraining herself, the acidity drying her fingertips, dulling her teeth: "yes, yes!"

But he sure had seen the orange, that clever one! and was laughing:

"Sour oranges and limes decrease your passion"—the gladiator was laughing. And the grating noise was starting up again, each bristle withering. Because she had her nerves:

"You and your nerves." But he'd forgive, the good, the mysterious Mateus, locking himself in the bathroom.

One night Lucrécia cried a little, while the exhausted warrior was dreaming beside her. The night calm, even pleasant, and the sky starry. Afterward she couldn't even remember exactly when she'd fallen asleep, so that the next day came adding itself to her wealth.

Then she said with rage: I'm getting out of here.

In the hope that at least in São Geraldo "a street was a street, a church a church, and even horses wore bells," as Ana had said.

With surprise she saw that that man wanted nothing more than to follow her and add himself to his wife's city, he who didn't belong to any city.

So it was that a few days later a car was bringing the couple back to the township.

Leaping from the taxi, she looked at a São Geraldo that was—noisy? people laughing offensively. The cacophony of a gear.

And unexpectedly the rain falling on the now unfamiliar city, dampening it in ashes and sorrows ...

She standing holding her parcels, the drops running down her face. But suddenly spurred to action, running up the stairs, throwing the packages onto a chair—invading her old dusty room and opening like a gale the balcony window and looking.

The raincoats were going down Market Street.

And at dusk the woman sighted the hill in the pasture.

The black slope was rising in a fist over São Geraldo. The somber kingdom of the equines.

That's how she stayed, upright, inexpressible. Both facing each other through the rain, merely forewarned. Ah! exclaimed the woman giving herself over in jubilation. She seemed to hear the hoof of a horse in swift blows.

But not much time had passed and she was realizing that it had been with extreme effort that the hill had answered her.

Taking advantage of her absence, São Geraldo had advanced in some sense, and she was already not recognizing things. Calling them, they would no longer answer—accustomed to being called by other names.

Other gazes, not hers, had transformed the township. She also was no longer looking at the trinkets, the ones at her back.

The presence of the maid was altering the structure of the second floor, strange hands would touch the little stuffed bird, Mateus installed like a king in Ana's chair which was so simple.

And she putting off the moment to go for a walk by herself, forgetting him.

"When I can, I can; when I can't, I can't—that's my motto!" Mateus Correia said one morning.

And that's how she got to know him more and more.

She'd let herself be led by her husband as if she were the

foreigner in São Geraldo. They'd go out together for a stroll, he tall, with strong hips, the mustache, and that rigid space into which he seemed to fit, the air around him almost palpable — and she with the ribbons she was stubbornly wearing, even regarding with distaste the sobriety that was in fashion. Her hat with a veil, and that constant running to keep up with him, running with her veil. Only when her husband died of a heart attack did she understand that strength, regulated and of a hurried slowness, the complete setting down when he'd sit, without abandoning his erect demeanor. But sometimes Mateus Correia would get diabolically happy, rub his hands and, without saying why he was so happy, exclaim:

"My dear little Lucrécia, today let's do some nice grazing!"

"Grazing ..." he'd said. She'd quickly return to the word that reminded her of dreams of dreams, terror escaping the walls and living calmly, she happy.

Had he been the one who'd transformed São Geraldo into a restaurant scene? the two of them would go together, she nearly jumping all around him — who was walking slightly behind, serious, perfumed: looking at the women behind her, taking interest in the middle-aged ones. Had it been Mateus who'd transformed the township's inhabitants into middle-aged creatures? It didn't bother him that his wife noticed his covetous stares, but wouldn't allow more than that: the rest was the enormous private life of an outsider.

She was looking at him across the table, watching him spellbound. Oh, God, the wind of São Geraldo was saying quietly; but the second course was arriving. When they were heading back it was almost nice, the relief among the almond trees, and a recognition that she didn't know where to direct: she was looking at the hill in the pasture. But, if she forced her feelings, everything would close without doors, she herself blocked by sudden resistance: which had ended up giving her a permanent balance, a certain pride in living, and such a generalized wonder, so impenetrable that it didn't even have a next moment: she'd say: what a lovely night! and her mouth was merely amazed. What a lovely night, Mateus, and the shadow would descend more and more taming the things in the breeze.

Whatever used to be seen, had now spread invisibly throughout São Geraldo—the wind was rocking the branches in the shadow. And her commitment had spread through the whole world: she'd hear news on the radio—while jewels were being bought and sold, and great bales of cotton were piling up at noon: Mateus Correia would arrive for lunch, she breathing in the tanned skin of her husband, trying to guess what was going on? all around were the happy beginnings of spring, fashions changing, nails growing and getting clipped; civilization being erected, people strolling on summer nights—and she looking from the balcony.

Looking with her face aged and excited by fatigue, scrutinizing the arrival of her husband who on a Wednesday night had arrived late for dinner.

She was at the living room balcony, and behind her the machinery of the house was functioning with joy, the smoke breathing itself out from the stove—like an old story. Market Street full, however, of new lights and of new cars. Lucrécia was waiting for Mateus, plunging her face into the street, ai! she sighed on the second floor, trolleys and cars muffling the exclamation. Countless horns soft or branching out were filling the air of the house with noises, almost lights.

But through the muffled horns you could feel the pleasure of the streets like the fountains of a garden, the whistle of the policeman between the lampposts: something mechanical was happening in the world. And, behind her, the pair of socks drying on the chair. Ai, she was sighing with her face covered in powder, her husband wasn't coming, ai! her exposed face was saying.

And suddenly the discordant sound, a train derailing inside the clock tower, one!—whitewashed face—two!—the house fire—three! it was eight o'clock and Mateus wasn't coming! Her eyes were dry but the horns were weeping and from the street the smell of sugar and vinegar was rising.

How the township had been transformed! the sweat of the hot night was making clothes stick to the body, the exalted perfume of flour reaching up to the nose: everything waiting for rain.

In fact it was already raining. Widely spaced drops at first, and then, little by little, but already immeasurable, the whole world was raining—as far as you looked there was the furious and constant rain, the bathed streets were emptying out. The lights refreshed. Through the gutters the waters were running in a rush.

Seen from the height of a window the city was a danger.

Cars, with invisible drivers, were sliding in the water and suddenly changing direction, you couldn't say why. São Geraldo had lost any purpose and was now functioning all by itself. Trolleys on their tracks were muffling other noises, and certain things were seeming to move completely silent—an elegant car appeared, tranquil, and disappeared. In São Geraldo a daily life had been born that no outsider would notice. It was raining and times were bad, it was a full-on crisis.

But there was a glory that up to that point hadn't been reached. Indivisible by the inhabitants. If a murder took place,

São Geraldo was the one who'd murdered. Never had things belonged so much to things. A spring had been forever uncoiled, and the city was a crime.

This city is mine, the woman looked. How heavy it was.

A few minutes later the rain stopped. The wet sidewalks were smelling to high heaven, the remains of the morning fish were being dragged toward the gutters … the bakery had already turned off its lights, the stars were clean.

The door opened and Mateus Correia came in drenched. She ran and hid in the man's shoulders and he, surprised, smoothed his companion's hair with wet hands. He had been the one chosen for her necessary downfall, and he was the one who was saving her: the woman cried from nerves, had the resistance of this world started to wear her out? she was crying happy, for an instant freed from the duty with which she'd been born, that they'd transmitted to her halfway and that she'd certainly transmit without explanations halfway too, hiding in his shoulder against the glory of an exploding São Geraldo—and Mateus seemed to know much more than he was letting on, since he wasn't even trying to understand her; perfect, perfect, his wet hands upon her hair—she suffocated with happiness, suffering for having to love somebody else one day, since it had been foretold without explanations that she too would someday love with brutality, maybe to raise this city with yet another stone? the good husband, incomprehensible, she crying—there was no way around it, the woman was happy.

Meanwhile Mateus kept taking her to every new restaurant.

And the more restaurants that opened, the more guaranteed São Geraldo became. The abundance, the elegance, cigar smoke and hot dishes, they were such security! Lucrécia felt sorry for Ana Rocha Neves who was living on the farm and had never known what it's like to live in such luxury and to eat those rich meats.

Ah, if Ana could see how São Geraldo was progressing! By now Lucrécia was trying to like those changes, afraid to lose her footing in the city and never reach it again. They were eating in silence. The ingratiating wife flattering him and flattering things slavishly: it's good, huh? Mateus Correia would answer offended: well, of course! Which would silence her, even making her blush. She then tried another approach:

"But we don't even like eating out, right?"

"Maybe you don't, I do!" he answered sarcastic, humiliated. Not liking, would that destroy the superior order? Her husband was even letting her know that if he went to the restaurant by himself everything was different, convincing her so well that it seemed to Lucrécia that her presence was enough for things to be camouflaged: suffering, she'd interrupt him: look, a falling star! she said fawning over him, and it was a lie, who knows why. Back home, in the dark city, how tempestuous and hot happiness was.

In that time of happiness she always had lots of little wrinkles appearing, she'd keep up with the fashions in French magazines, mingling with that dusty era that aspired with suffocation toward posterity—while useful forms of thoughts were being employed: "in theory it's great but not in practice," this was said a lot, and in the light of a streetlamp the car was passing at full speed.

The next day, in the late afternoon, the two weeks of fine rain had ceased at last.

The prosperous city was glowing. On the sidewalks a few men raised indecisive faces: the sky was bright, almost green, almost neutral … And under the sharpness of the colorlessness the modest rooftops of São Geraldo were rising. For a rare moment, beneath the final illuminated raindrops, the city was unanimous. People were looking while blinking, recognizing the steadfastness of things. Their faces surprised as if warned that the hour had come. To turn their backs on the mature city, and leave forever.

Also the word "society" was being used a lot, in those days. "Society demands everything and gives nothing back, isn't that right, sir?," was said a lot.

"Society demands everything and gives nothing back," Mateus said on that Saturday morning, in the middle of the conversation that both seemed to have been seeking for so long.

In fact they wanted finally to face off. And when by chance they started talking about husbands cheating on their wives, they both seized with gratitude the opportunity. She made herself comfortable with her sewing on her lap.

"It's not considered a crime at all," he said, "that's how society is made," he added with pride, his eyes moist with emotion because he was so good.

"Yes it is," she said attentive.

"That's how society is made," the man repeated with fore-thought. "It's not a crime for a man to have some interest in women but it's a crime for the wife to be interested in another man."—Such good sense and logic he had! both were hovering over neutral ground, neither wanting to be the first to take a chance.

"Right."

"I never dishonored the home I created," said the husband and they stared at each other afraid he'd gone too far—Mateus had used some wrong word. A certain fatigue had in fact overcome her, she was almost slipping into a sincerity that would make their superior conversation unbearable. She was straightening out the tablecloth, smoothing down a crease.

"The home I created I never dishonored!" the man repeated suddenly quite loud, as if changing the arrangement of the same words would make him more comfortable.

He won't let it go, his wife was thinking. Ah, if she had someone to tell about this afterwards, how truthful she'd suddenly be and how she'd harm that man she didn't know but knew how to wound.

She wanted her husband to stop talking but Mateus now irrepressible kept going explaining his character, his moral principles and his way of treating women—though none of this revealed him for a single moment. She was rolling up the edge of the tablecloth, daydreaming.

"Lucrécia," her husband said with a certain anguish, "you're not listening!"

"Yes I am, you were saying you'd be polite to women in any situation."

"Yes, in any situation," Mateus repeated disappointed …

They fell silent. She was looking at the floor without interest. He, on the other hand, excited by the nobility with which he'd described himself, was gazing avidly at his hands, restless and full of plans for the future. In fact he was realizing that speaking was his best way of thinking and that it was good to be listened to by a woman. He tried to start the conversation back up but Lucrécia was fleeing with a demeanor that seemed to him calm and sad.

Looking at her Mateus might have discovered that deep down he'd always been scared of her. There was nothing more dangerous than a cold woman. And Lucrécia was chaste as a fish. For the first time he seemed to notice in his wife's face a certain helpless abandonment. He averted his eyes with kindness.

"And you, what are your plans?" he asked in order to please her, forgetting that he'd only thought of his own.

"Come again?" she awoke, "what plans? which? what are you talking about?"

He himself was spooked without knowing why:

"Nothing … you know, Lucrécia, plans, projects, you know …"

"What do you mean by projects?" his wife was demanding with irony. "What do you mean by that, do you have some plan for us?"

"What plans for us?"

"But, Mateus, didn't you mention plans for us?"

"No, it wasn't for us … I mean, yes, but I don't know what you're imagining, it was all well-intentioned …"

"Well-intentioned!"

"Yes, well-intentioned! why would there need to be bad intentions, my God!"

"But who mentioned anything bad? so things were bad between us," she said stridently.

"No, it wasn't that … I mean plans for you …"

"… you think I should have plans separate from yours?"

"No, for God's sake, I also have my own but you …"

"… separate from mine?"

"Oh my God!"

"What are yours, Mateus."

Thus put on the spot he couldn't say what they were. And he was looking straight ahead incommunicable, halted with stubbornness along the way.

"They're mine," he said with pride and suffering.

"And might one know what they are?"

"To progress," Mateus Correia finally said with effort and shame.

She opened her mouth and stared at him with enormous astonishment.

After a moment, the whole house took up its position on the street, and, defeated inside the dining room, she said:

"Yes, Mateus."

"Don't you think so?" he got excited, and, without knowing that her husband would die of a heart attack, she was afraid of his joy. "And don't believe it's just something in the air, I've got it all written down in my head, ok? tell me what you think, ok?"

"About what?"

"But about what I said, what the devil, Lucrécia!" the wounded fighter exclaimed.

"How am I supposed to know what you said," she mumbled full of rage and despair ...

It was the only time they faced off.

The beauty of all this is that she was so lost that she seemed to be guided. Rich and lost, the cinemas opening, the mirrors multiplying the spots. His asking, her responding, and a certain lack of control: she really couldn't hold back certain phrases.

"I'm going to buy some sheer fabric for a blouse embroidered with cross-stitches!"

She had to tell him.

"It's been so long since I've had a banana," and she was almost grabbing Mateus by the lapel, he turning away uncomfortable. "A fabulous assortment of jewelry, Mateus! Mateus! my lips are opening," she was informing him.

Until one day she said in the middle of a room full of guests:

"Rigoletto is always Rigoletto," she said.

And she was startled. Could this be a pronouncement from another age? so much so that if there were young people in the room they'd look at her oddly. Lucrécia guessed it with fear.

São Geraldo was no longer at its starting point, she had lost her old importance and her inalienable place in the township. There were even plans to build a viaduct to connect the hill to the lower city … The plots on the hill were already beginning to be sold for future residences: where would the horses go?

Watching the arrival of men and machines, the horses were patiently shifting the position of their hooves. Shooing off the sunlit flies with their tails.

During this period Lucrécia Correia finally merged with what was happening. Ending up by admitting that she'd dreamed of this progress and had given it her own strength. Recognizing here and there traces of her construction.

She then started her strolls again, and a new firmness toward her husband was born. At this time he'd already started to work less and would occasionally spend hours at home, bored. And if both made up their minds not to go out, they'd constantly bump into each other in the rooms with irritation. One of them would need to be expelled, now that Lucrécia had recovered her former power. At the table he'd toss little balls he made from breadcrumbs that his wife would receive on her serious face, or crumple a sheet of newspaper, throwing the ball at her head:

"I'll split your tarantella in two"—he called someone's head a tarantella. She'd blanch.

By the time she reached the front door she was happier, opening her parasol in a dry snap, balancing on the tightrope.

How well-equipped São Geraldo was. Ready to sail away? But where would that thing sail that, because it was of stone, had made its glory.

When she'd return, she'd find him smoking, on edge. As soon as he saw her come in, he'd put out the cigarette, circling it, tracking it down, and, with a pleasure for his foot: stepping straight on it, right on its light. Both would stare dazzled at the shredded cigarette. She stunned as if he'd just killed a rooster.

Things kept getting testier between people and even Mateus, who didn't belong to the township, was withering with irritation. He'd head toward the window and say, as if ordering his wife to stay—because Lucrécia's somehow victorious presence was suffocating him:

"Ok then. I'm going to see a little star."

Lucrécia was the only one no longer affected by the tension of the city. Especially when someone would complain of the difficulty of getting a trolley or renting a house, Lucrécia Correia would lower her eyes trying to hide—that it was her fault.

But if she went to the doctor she'd turn chatty, getting mixed up with ever more precise and difficult expressions:

"It's not quite pain, it's more of an impression, doctor, and then I don't feel anything, for months—it doesn't quite get to be unpleasant, you understand?—Ah, and I also get chills for no reason," she'd add after a while with haughtiness.

The doctor would listen, pretending to think. With his drowsy face he'd punctuate that woman's every sentence. Oh, she was peculiar and irritating. São Geraldo was now full of a certain kind of woman who liked going to the doctor. Lucrécia had in fact put on her best dress. And now she was waiting modestly for the verdict. "Rest, ma'am, lots of rest." She left imperious, calm.

"Give me that embroidery, Mateus!," she'd mumble hiding her strength.

And even with her concealing her claws, Mateus was shrinking more and more.

It wasn't only her fault. Amidst the confusion of the city is where you'd spot an outsider: he had nothing to cling to, whereas Lucrécia Neves was part of the avalanche. She'd prepared it moment by moment. After she'd taken her husband to live on Market Street, she'd grown progressively meaner. Mateus would stay home all day, gazing from his window at the bright shop windows on rainy days, counting the cars. He was always hunting down broken things to fix and would sleep after lunch, on those dirty afternoons full of wind. While she'd strut through the rooms dragging her "robe de chambre." She thought she was the most intelligent creature in the world and made a point of proving it to Mateus. He, with an ever-weaker voice in an ever-larger body, exasperated her, setting off those short kicks in the tail of her house dress. She'd look at him with wide astonished eyes, laugh loudly with coldness:

"My dear little Mateus," she'd say smashing him with curiosity, "my dear, little, skinny-legged Mateus," she'd say laughing and taking advantage of the outsider's weakness in order to expel him.

He'd laugh a lot because these were the kind of little games he'd taught his wife back when he was the man of the house; he'd laugh approvingly and they'd look at each other. But she was feeling a bit at the mercy of the man who'd seen her decline before her rebirth. Proud, she didn't want witnesses to the way she'd tried to transform herself and to how she'd employed the same dirty scaffolding that São Geraldo used before turning up with a new building or a more modern sewage system. The more she feared being in his hands, the more she'd try to please him. She'd put on a flattering and odious demeanor that her husband would accept swelling for a moment with his former virility: she'd say to him as if speaking of a third person:

"He doesn't know anything about clothes! dress his wife in burlap and tell him: it's beautiful! he'll repeat: it's beautiful!" — she'd laugh and her husband would laugh while being fawned over; then she'd laugh more softly: the idiot.

She had to keep the hilarity going in order to disguise the word, while through his own laughter he, modest and troubled, was already examining his wife. Lucrécia, not satisfied, risking everything, would repeat: the idiot. They'd look at each other laughing so much that tears would appear in their eyes, her laughter interspersed with strident "ai"s.

The more São Geraldo expanded, the harder she found it to speak clearly, so dissembled she'd become. Mateus, now extremely curious, would ask her: "how was the visit?" — she immediately on guard: "I don't know, so-so!"

"Is the house big?" he'd insist, eager, in his slippers.

"Who knows, it's appropriate ...," she'd defend herself looking at him with intensity to figure out whether his questions would become more pressing.

"But how many rooms?"

"You think I noticed ... I swear I didn't even look, what a question ..."

"But anyway, a single living room?"

"Two," she finally said, gentle and worn out.

It seemed to her that the only way now to describe São Geraldo was to get lost in its streets.

Until Mateus was reading a passage from that day's paper. She was hearing almost intimidated his heroic tone — an outsider could sing this big city that was taking shape, whereas she no longer even knew how to see it …

"The public," Mateus was reading, "followed these fortunate renovations with interest, and our press did not fail to applaud them, emphasizing the moral achievement of such actions. For, is it not by valuing the legacy of our ancestors, built with the sweat of their brow, that a city is honored?", Mateus Correia was trembling. She would have liked to interrupt the tone of insufferable beauty with which her husband was reading the tributes to the city. "But the Urbanization Committee recently had the unfortunate idea of demolishing the old Posts and Telegraphs building, the kind of idea that makes the stones of our streets shake with indignation. Needless to say the people of São Geraldo await explanations." Gradually, as the man was declaiming, Lucrécia Neves was becoming enlarged, enigmatic, a statue at whose feet, during civic festivals, flowers would be placed.

Then she'd go out alone, enjoying the city traffic with suffering, paying attention to everything: roads full of dust and sunlight, the people passing by. Her difficulty stripped the immediate interest from things, with effort she was going far away in search of whatever existed, taking enormous and useless strolls from which she'd return exhausted. Mateus! she'd yell irritated, Mateus! come here! Mateus already deafened, she awaiting his response, and the house half in shadow, tidy. Mateus!, she'd order, and kept getting more engrossed, dominated by the motionlessness of the rooms, plunged into a reality that could only be overtaken by flights, and from which she could only tear herself away with brutality: Mateus!

Soon enough that state of affairs even seemed to have always existed, the house half in darkness in that rich period of winter. The roads were being covered with asphalt before the rains came, the lights were coming on earlier, the doors opening and closing dryly, Mateus asking from one room to the next: what day is it today? and his own voice answering: Tuesday.

That was when she took the picture that would later so intrigue her children.

During this period she was really at her peak.

She sat, nicely controlled her neck muscles, her vision darkened with emotion, the photographer let out a cry: smile! the magnesium exploded in brightness. Done, the photographer said, and her face, shoulders and waist had crumbled.

Days later she went to pick up the result. And behold that recognizable, hard woman. Was her face saying some thing? her thought was pointing some thing out, her neck tense. A picture like one you take in a big city, which São Geraldo still wasn't. It had been a harbinger.

She hung it in the hallway, beside a postcard-sized drawing of the future viaduct. She'd dust it daily. Sometimes, dropping her embroidery, she'd run over and halt before it. Both looking at each other. She staring at it with stupor and pride: what a fully realized work. She'd even become freer after being photographed; she now seemed able to be whatever she wanted.

But more and more the photograph was growing detached from the model, and the woman would seek it as if seeking an ideal. The face on the wall, so swollen and dignified, had in the suffocating dream a destiny, whereas she herself ... Perhaps she'd fallen into the machinery of things, and the picture was the unreachable surface, already the superior order of solitude—her own history that, unnoticed by Lucrécia Neves, the photographer had captured for posterity.

10   The Corn in the Field

ON ONE OF HIS FINAL BUSINESS TRIPS, INSTEAD OF leaving his wife on Market Street, Mateus rented the little house on the island for her, hoping the sea would give her some color.

The ferry was lingering while surmounting the waves that a frustrated storm was filling with rage and foam.

Pale from nausea Lucrécia was squinting making an effort to see from afar the land that was holding back. She'd hardly disembarked however, and a certain pleasure was already emerging with her feet sinking into the sand by the dock. Soon she was nearing the center of the small seaside city, directing the entourage of porter and maid. Before taking the carriage she also saw the sign for Dr. Lucas, who represented, in Mateus's eyes, the assurance of Lucrécia's health, for she really had lost weight.

Climbing into the carriage, she took careful note of the house where she'd find the doctor if she needed him. With surprise her heart instead of feeling merely confident, did it shiver awakening to the memory of an almost whole strength? she gave the order to depart.

The horses were carrying her in fits and sudden starts along the path but soon were running with raised heads—and soon the woman wanted them to fly. Weakened by some desire she even pulled off her hat and let her hair be tousled in the wind. What she meant by this gesture only the trees witnessed, and the horses were advancing among them.

There was the wooden house, in black and white because of the moisture that was darkening its outlines. The surrounding foliage was singed by the sea air that the constant wind was blowing: Lucrécia was smelling the salty air, cautiously sniffing it all which seemed to her to have a cold and quick reality like a stream's—and which so reminded her of the silent time before the progress of São Geraldo. A slight house, built on sandy soil; after a few days she noticed that she too was waking up with white skin and black lashes, all in light and dark, so much had she already begun to imitate the new landscape. A sparrow had crossed the small room from one window to the other. Lucrécia Correia never wearied of wandering through the miniscule dwelling, more and more astonished: everything had become so easy that it hurt a little.

At the first excuse, because of a missing cheese, she'd fought with the maid and dismissed her. And finally—alone with her former careful way of living—she'd notice each creak of wood, keep an eye on the roses growing in the garden, do quick laps and give sharp cries of recognition. At night the cut roses would dimly illuminate the bedroom and leave the woman sleepless; the waters beating on the distant beach wanted to transport her but the croaking of frogs was monitoring her from close by. In the morning she'd awake as pale as if she'd been riding horseback all night: she'd run barefoot and open the door to the sandy yard. New roses had blossomed.

The sea was far off but the roses would burn in the salty wind that blew in the late afternoon.

She'd then sit in the doorway of the house with Ana's shawl on her shoulders. As night approached everything would seem farther off, whoever had left had left for good, the branches would tremble, the trees would blacken in their roots and the sandy clearings would show themselves to be: white. It was an immense place. If some thing were to happen, it would ring out in bells. The woman was even avoiding joy, hesitating in those steps that she'd recognize only through the intermediary of dread: she'd bring in the chair, close the house and light the lamp on the table. Everything that had been outside was inside.

She'd fall asleep watchful as if dawn could find the house surrounded by horses. And it would resemble the first night of sleep after someone was buried. Had it been that pause in the revolution that had one day frightened Ana? The tick-tock of the alarm clock was dangling every thing at its own surface. Giving every object a precise solitude. The egg on the kitchen table was egg-shaped. The square of the window was square. And in the morning the shape of the woman in the doorway was dark in the light.

And the mosquitos. The house of roses was lifted in glory into the air by slight mosquitos with tall legs. They had grown oversized and, weakened by this excess, it was easy to touch them: when you left a glass of water out they'd drown without at least deteriorating. It was a brief life, without resistance. They seemed to live off a history much larger than their own. And, useless and resplendent as they were, they would make of the world the orb.

*

The spider had already woven several webs in the window when the woman headed down the road that would take her to the center of town.

Tiled houses were at the water's edge and the whole small city was arrayed in a line for anyone approaching from the sea. Behind the line heaped-up things were decaying in heat and slavery, the women at the windows looking at the rare clouds or keeping an eye on the wooden gangplank that connected the land to the boats.

At night the sea would darken, the gangplank whiten, and bottle rockets would shoot up and explode above the rooftops waking people up. Until the silence of the late night would return and you could make out the calming slaps of water.

That was when the lighthouse would begin its patrol and with patience pick out between intervals the objects from the darkness. In the morning the tide had gone out, the day was being born fresh, windy. But gradually the island would dry out again and by ten o'clock it was a dry city—the gangplank was burning, upon it travelers were looking around dimmed on empty stomachs: the streets lay parched.

All this Lucrécia saw, with one foot upon the village. This her auspicious land.

Wherever a city was forming, there she would be building it: the electrical wiring in the bar was wrapped in fine red paper and the old lady on her knees was washing the stairs. Coffee with milk, Lucrécia said to her, serious, with pleasure.

And nearly at dusk, tired of walking around, she saw finally Dr. Lucas's office open and from it a man emerge with a heavy gait. He seemed to her quite aged yet as calm as she'd remembered him. The woman quickly crossed the sidewalk and stood before him laughing quietly.

In the half-darkness she didn't see his surprise but heard his muffled voice mumbling her name and she grew serious for still being that person they could call: Lucrécia Neves from São Geraldo.

They took a walk through the city park just as they'd walked through the park in the township. The doctor was pointing out to her the public monuments ... And from afar the sanatorium where his wife now lived, forcing him to relocate his practice to the island.

Lucrécia was strolling beside him, the small city darkening dizzily, the lights finally came on. The doctor even ended up buying her a little bag of bonbons, Lucrécia was looking uneasily at the dark sky.

She spoke to him of Mateus, of the house on Market Street, in the night that the sea was filling with salt, but nothing was reaching its own end, the breeze was bringing and taking away the words and the lampposts were being deformed in the water.

Doctor Lucas calm as a man who really worked. It was somehow humiliating to realize that, strong and hardly talkative, he was neither revealing nor concealing himself. To the doctor Lucrécia didn't need to mention the blouse she was planning to embroider; she'd always imitated her men.

Maybe the house of roses was just a beginning and on this very night she'd come to know another order ... and she was already wanting to touch all of this, once again came the uncertainty about what Doctor Lucas might do, and she was trying to figure it out by watching him, as if the night that was falling could help her with its darkness.

When he went to assist her with her coat, and while he was

brushing his arm across her shoulders—for just an instant Lu-crécia Neves leaned back ... had he made her arms more lively? had he noticed? or was she imagining it? out of uncertainty the hazy light of a lamppost lit up, the instant turning gold in the night, out of uncertainty and delight the little lady was breath-ing observing severely the car that was moving ahead over the irregular stones: the wheels were screeching and Doctor Lucas was speaking about what he'd done that day, she interrupting him with her errant mouth:

"Doctor Lucas, Doctor Lucas, you work too much, sir!" she was saying taking the opportunity to touch his clothes.

The doctor, with tired and vibrant eyes, was laughing at her ...

"Ah!" mumbled the woman.

"What happened ..."

"That star," she said with tears in her eyes in a sincerity that, in search of expression, was making her lie. "It's just that I turned around and saw the star," she said bathed by the grace of her lie.

This time the doctor looked at her through the darkness.

She blushed. But he was also looking at her with under-standing and strength, leading her now with a first firmness through the dark lane, and avoiding touching her.

A moment more and, not touching, they were both thrown off balance, not touching was almost bringing them to a certain extreme point. Everything had become precious as if Lucrécia Neves Correia were holding such heavy things with her left hand: a low branch almost undid the bun in her hair, stealing from her a slightly painful exclamation of rapture.

"See," he said with clarity and strength, "on such a lovely

night I'll have to work"—through the darkness he was looking at her, imposing on her severely a more dignified attitude …

"… impossible!" she yelled shattered, her happy chest lighting up without paying attention to the man's warning. "Impossible to work so much," she added foolishly.

"Can you see all right?" asked the doctor imperiously.

He wanted to take responsibility for what he had unleashed, and did he look guilty? she obeyed with her mouth half-opened.

"Here we are"—the jammed door was cracking open and the man smiled—"did the walk do you any good?" he asked in another tone.

"It did, doctor."

Was the doctor angry? The frogs were croaking hoarsely.

"I don't know how to thank you, doctor …"—she was speaking with effort, with an ardor slightly out of place, her hair fluttering.

"Don't thank me then," he responded curtly.

Oh how annoyed he was!

"Yes, doctor."

Through the darkness dimly illuminated by the proximity of the sea he looking at her now curious, almost amused—finally smiling:

"Well then, good-night, get some rest."

He reached out his hand thinking to meet hers and accidentally touched her arm—she blanched: "good night," she answered, and the man walked off stepping on leaves.

Lucrécia Correia was lingering at the door, held at her current height by the scattered frogs. She coughed snuggling into her coat. She kicked away a bit of rubbish.

Then she went into the house and turned on the light. Inside everything was lightweight, blown. The bed, the table, the lamp. Nothing could be touched—the slight and upright extremities in the wind. Why don't I go over and touch them? she couldn't and yawned, shivery.

Then she changed clothes and lay down. A gentle joy was already starting to circulate in her blood with the first warmth, her teeth were once again sharpening and her nails hardening, her heart finally becoming precise in beats hard and curt. She succumbing to an extreme fatigue that no man would love. Fatigue and remorse and horror, insomnia that the lighthouse was haunting in silence.

She didn't want to take the path of love, it would be a too-bloody reality, the rats—the lighthouse lit her in a flash and revealed the unknown face of lust. In the phosphorescence of the darkness she was seeing once again the ballrooms immobilized in the light, and the horrified people dancing completely still, an automaton reality and pleasure—the woman withdrew pale, ah! she was saying surprised.

But gradually, the lighthouse illuminating and darkening her, she started losing her mind imagining a conversation in which Doctor Lucas would seem even more severe, she even humbler, asking him, to buy time, a thousand questions that would be a dance around him, destined to confound the man's strength: sir, do you like big houses? sir, do you believe in me? if I were about to die would you save me, sir? do you speak many languages, sir? that's wonderful! and quickly showing him her things: here's my house for the time being, this city looks so much like São Geraldo! That's my window.

So much shyness didn't come from shame, it came from beauty, from fear, she back again with the great frogs.

But suddenly humble, hard, smoothing out the tablecloth to make the vision come easier: I'll give you my life and nothing more. Doctor Lucas, one couldn't make up the expression he'd have just then, crying out: I want less than your life, I want you! Her responding with pain, with modesty: when it comes to love it's undignified to ask for so little, buddy.

Once the tensest moment of the night had passed some streak of humidity was finally broken, the waves were beating softly. The woman nodded off and Doctor Lucas mumbled a bit ridiculously with his somber face: so you don't know how to be free. And her answering: ah, I can't, you know, and she ended up free, so much that she fell asleep.

The next day she was waiting for him on the sidewalk in front of his office.

When he saw her he stopped short with the key in his hand, his lips pressed tight. He was irritated.

But she was looking at him patient, modest; night was falling.

Without speaking Lucas closed the door of his office and they went off together. They were walking around the small city immersed in shadow. The woman would sometimes walk ahead, and Doctor Lucas would stop. She'd then go on ahead fatigued in the park, making sure with a quick glance that he was still observing her; she'd go on, stumble, lean in perdition on the stone eagles running her fingers over the reliefs … He was watching mute—while Lucrécia Neves was displaying herself, trying to make herself understood in the only way she had to speak, displaying with monotonous perseverance; he becoming a harder man while watching; she carrying on silently, spinning around in front of him, working him with patience in order to form her counterpart in this world, looking at the low sky.

Until, already out of the center of town, they saw a closed house. The dry ivy was climbing the columns, the blinds covered in dust were shut. Near the counter the broken pitcher. Lucas wanted to go ahead, but what did she wish to show him in the abandoned house? the woman didn't know and persisted trusting in her own ignorance; the ground of dry leaves was muffling her steps. She ended up pushing the wooden gate. But Lucas had halted stubbornly. Don't be afraid, she was saying with a protective glance, it was just a silent dwelling. There was the crack in the wall. Could that be the house's horror?

They went on. He belonging to his wife while, without getting discouraged, Lucrécia Neves was spinning around him; and the more the man was catching on, the more inscrutable he was becoming. Sometimes the woman would realize he was feeling the urge to get rid of her, he was so annoyed. But she'd keep on gently provoking him, with a resignation that would sometimes make her think she'd been walking in the dust for years without a single breeze to bring relief to the air. She was very tired. Eventually there was established between them at last a short and brusque relationship whose possibilities they wouldn't know how to measure: Lucas would take out a cigarette, she'd remove with insufferable gentleness the lighter from his hand, Lucas holding back a movement of repulsion; she'd light the small flame conquering him, he conquered but increasingly gruff: when she'd give him back the lighter, they'd go on.

One night they were standing on the hill that so resembled the hill in the pasture—until the dawn took on a sharp stained-glass tone; he with his dark face.

It was at this time that Lucas began to be scared. When the light of the lighthouse would pass over them it revealed two unknown faces. Lucrécia Neves unknown, yes, but at peace, concentrated on her utmost surface. Sometimes a rapid contraction would pass over her face as if a fly had landed upon it. Then she'd move her hooves, patient. He unknown but already anxious, looking around, placing his hand on the trunk of the chestnut ... Then Lucrécia placed her hand on the trunk of the chestnut. Through the tree Lucrécia was touching him. The indirect world.

Loving him, returning to the necessity of that gesture that was pointing things out and, with the same single movement, creating whatever there was of the unknown inside them—all of her was on the verge of that gesture when she was touching the trunk his hand was touching—just as she'd looked at a household object in order to reach the city: humble, touching whatever she could. For the first time she was tempting him through herself, and through the overvaluation of that small part of individuality that until now had not surpassed itself nor brought her to love of herself. But now, with a final effort, she was tempting solitude. Solitude with a man: with a final effort, she was loving him.

Then she returned by the footpaths that were dawning. She'd never seen the house of roses at sunrise. At that hour it was brittle, not very intimate. And so superficial. Every corner was visible.

The days moreover were marvelous at that time of year. Autumn was beginning and in the windows spider webs were shining. Distances had become much greater though easy to cover. To the woman it really seemed like living on the line of the horizon. It was from there that she would see each small thing with its lights, this strange world where you could uselessly touch everything. The roosters would crow behind the houses. As for the mornings, they were for throwing a shoe into the distance—and the dog running after it barking. It was hunting season.

In fact restless bitches were advancing without owners among the bamboo on the beach.

While Lucas was working, Lucrécia would go on lots of walks. The countryside dotted with small gleamings, with black streaks—and the cow ... The cow looking at an expanse with one eye, the opposite expanse with the other eye; head-on would be so easy, but the cow never saw. Lucrécia Neves Correia, the butterflies—and the cow. On a bigger rock she could make out the ants quite nicely. They were black. And later the cloud.

The woman's head was peering at the field. There was a thing that her mind didn't grasp and that a horse would see—this was the easy name of things. Even the grottos were green ... there was no darkness in which to hide. Everything was expelling her from solitude—the ripe sapodillas.

And in the morning, opening the window, how inhospitable the brightness was. Piles and piles of wood were burned and smoke emerged; the bees. Near the beach Lucrécia's skin was turning green in the light of the waves. The woman was then sneezing. There was no other way to be.

Until one afternoon she decided to take a walk in the prairie. That silence. But fear was substituted by hope. And not even her solitude could keep itself going because ... why was the corn already high? she was searching with her eyes for whatever was keeping her from being alone—farther on the ears of corn were shaking, heavy: the corn in the field was her most interior life. The field stretched out silent; there was the other life.

But looking at those lands where the spirit still was free,

"what! unutilized plots in this day and age!" on top of it the practical woman thought with stubbornness: "Here. Here I would build a great city."

There really was room and, tearing out the weeds and the corn, the ground would be so to speak ready. Then, in her other life, with effort, she'd make houses arise, bridges crisscross heaving, ghost factories function. A city she'd call São Geraldo? beginning it again with patience, this time without abandoning it for an instant with her attention—until reaching the point where the township was, in order to recognize, beneath the sedimentation, the true names of things.

But at dusk the sun would pale. And over the imagined city the wind started to blow stronger and to whirl around the ears of corn wrapping them in shadow. Is it going to rain? the woman thought hurrying back, she'd barely have time to meet Doctor Lucas—but the wind was running faster than her steps, pushing her skirt ahead, uncovering her nape blinding her face with her hair, she, for whom it hadn't been enough for the corn to grow.

It was on that night that while looking at Lucas—maybe because she needed him once again—she imagined the man was finally starting to yield. Just for a second: because in the dark and wind wouldn't that animal face be impassioned?

But would it be passion or hunger for mercy? Since in the dark she was seeing him the way she'd see an animal—it was a bull's head or a dog's—the head of a man. Of a man who grazed in the field and chewed grass, and who bit off high leaves along the way—and who at night would stop in the wind—empty, potent, king of the animals—the head in the dark.

Could this be the dementia of solitude? king of the animals. Nauseated, she'd have wanted to turn around and leave, such did she still prefer the promising confusion of words to this nudity without beauty, to this truth of hospitals and war. Never had her back been so against the wall.

Averting her eyes with distaste: she didn't even love him, the wind was murmuring in the trees. But an instant later, from weariness, growing heavy and without a will of her own: oh a woman for that man. She was strong, crude, patient—without expecting anything in return she belonged to that resigned head of a beast, and from this other animal she would await without curiosity the order to go ahead or halt, dragging herself sweaty, resisting as best she could. In order at night to raise her head beside the animal's head, both chewing in silence in the dark, both surviving as an obscure victory.

Maybe even this was to belong to God. For they had said that man would eat bread with the sweat of his brow and that women would have children in pain. You couldn't even say she loved him, it was so lacking in glory. Standing face to face, without malice, without sex, clinging to the somber joy of subsisting.

Though that woman's strange response was still: I prefer to live in the city. And there was no way to criticize her for not seizing the chance to belong to a man, and not to things. In fact he'd offered nothing, he'd just been a head expressing itself in the dark. They would make concrete every thought about bridges, every idea about a railway. One was however waiting for the other to guess it, the utmost of giving and accepting, there'd never been such a need to be understood. Nothing was being demanded but this instant of survival, that's how it was, that's how it would be.

The next night—she awaiting him at his office door, both spent by insomnia—Lucas finally said it was impossible.

Lucrécia was shocked as if unaware what this was all about,

and he seeing so much fake innocence got mad. The woman started to cry, softly at first — she really did seem surprised by his haste — saying she'd been forever wounded, that everything had been ruined forever, though both hardly knew what "everything" she was referring to; that she'd expected from him "some enormous thing, oh Doctor Lucas," and that he'd wounded her forever, she was repeating amidst tears and syllables swallowed by sobs. The man was looking at her with brutality, seeing her crying mixing up her words; she seemed pure and puritan. He said severely like a doctor: calm down. The weeping subsided immediately. She wiped her eyes and blew her nose.

But without tears she was horrible to look at. Her mouth so painted. Her face in the darkness was anonymous, repugnant, fantastic. The doctor fell silent confronted with this truth that had taken, to the surprise of his eyes, the form of a face. He wanted to ask how he'd wounded her but this no longer mattered; when he saw her face without disguise he knew he'd wounded her somehow. He also noticed that the woman hadn't complained about any single fact. Except about himself, which was as vague as it was serious and accusatory; he'd been struck.

Lucrécia was now keeping absent in the shadow, he couldn't see her nor did he know whom to address when he said in an empty and dry tone:

"I don't know what I'm to blame for but I ask forgiveness." — The light of the lighthouse revealed them so quickly that they couldn't see each other. — "I ask forgiveness for not being a 'star' or 'the sea'" — he said ironically — "or for not being something that gives itself," he said blushing. "I ask forgiveness for not knowing how to give myself even to myself — until now I've only been asked for kindness — but never to … — in order to give myself in this way I'd lose my life if necessary—but again I ask forgiveness, Lucrécia: I don't know how to lose my life."

It had been his longest speech to date, and the most embarrassing. He'd spoken with difficulty and now was withdrawing into the dark. Was he understanding, more than she did, that Lucrécia might have been wanting just a gesture? asking for a feeling and nothing more? he was afraid that this was so little. Fear, beside this weak being who didn't die: because he was so paltry that, when his strength ran out, he himself would die. He looked at his hands in the dark. He was making out thick fingers, the bones, the wide back of his hand. Sensitivity was only in the web of veins. What is she asking of me? he was wondering looking at the hands that were his strength, what's she asking of me? and his austerity was as insufferable as the night air seemed free. He loosened his collar, moved his neck toward the sky. Coolness was blowing amongst the trees, he'd grown used to understanding just the words; now, whatever had no words was understood with square hands, and with steps that wouldn't halt even if his heart were struck, he who never was mortally struck, such was his impotence.

Thus, walking down the footpaths back to town—he wasn't thinking about Lucrécia Neves. He was also hardly feeling the humidity of the night; he was walking serious, without future.

And Lucrécia too … But no, beneath her futility she was working with time running out as in war. He wasn't feeling sorry for himself or for Lucrécia. He was calm, strong. Because he was a man—if you wanted with effort to sum him up, not counting his unknown nights and his work—he was a slow, sincere man and didn't feel sorry for himself. That had never helped anyway. It would make things easier to think he was weak. But no, he was strong. Which hadn't stopped Lucrécia from rattling him, making him wonder now where his own guilt lay. Which became so great that there was no longer any punishment.

Individual life? the dangerous thing is that each person was dealing with centuries.

Several generations before him had already been expelled from a colony and delivered to solitude; and, if the man had cut off the self-love that this solitude would bring him, that was because his awareness, and more than awareness, a memory, was still making him at least hide the joy of being alone. Now however it was no longer a question of protecting himself. It was a question of losing himself until reaching the minimum of himself, throbbing spot that Lucrécia Neves had almost awoken—and at last he'd no longer need to be anonymous in order to conceal his pride, at last, maybe, he'd no longer need to be such a good doctor—because in that minimum of himself he would already be there entire ... what danger. The doctor coughed pretending. Those who were yet to come might assail him with a new way of laughing ... Everything he was telling himself would come to pass, the man was trembling without feeling sorry for himself. The frogs were croaking, he wiped his mouth with his handkerchief.

What to make of Lucrécia, what to make of his wife who was embroidering in the sanatorium and would ask for red thread and lift her head hopefully when her husband arrived. And of Lucrécia? some tiny emphasis seemed to be Lucrécia's only destiny, vehemence her only strength. Even before dying she was one of the raptured souls who even a tough man inhales in the air of the nights.

And Lucrécia's, was that the true surrendered life? the one that gets lost, the waves that rise furiously over the rocks, the mortal fragrance of flowers—and there was the sweet evil, the boulders now submerged by the waves, and in Lucrécia's innocence was *evil*, she waiting far away in the wind from the hill, waiting, sweet, dizzying, with her impure breath of roses, her neck crushable by one of his hands—she, waiting down through the centuries, decrepit and a child, for him to heed at last the plea of the waves over the rocks and, leaping over the tallest escarpment of the night, unleash a howl, the long neigh with which he'd respond to the beauty and perdition of this world: who hadn't seen on windless nights how cruel and murderous the silver flowers were?

Stopped on the path, the man's gaze was withdrawing cunningly, and he himself was moving forward with extreme caution among the branches—hunched, ready to leap. He wanted to reply, no longer to Lucrécia who was calling him—quickly he'd surpassed her, and if he were to speak he'd finally have managed to reply to a venetian blind flapping in the silence of a street, to a mirror that reflects, to everything that up till now we leave without an answer.

A breath of wind almost woke him. Lucas was startled as he looked at his big hands that were turning in front of his bestialized face, his naïve hands that had created the metamorphosis—with a certain horror he was staring at them, reduced to whatever sufficed of himself, and he'd cry out in victory and pain because it was the first vertigo of a man.

And would he no longer be ashamed of miracles? Would the constant threat cease that even the perfume might say "that there," and that the shape of a hand might repeat it … Finally, finally wounded, mortally wounded, what peace.

He'd waited his whole life for the moment in which he'd finally be lost. What rotting in the wet leaves.

He stopped again. The lighthouse was scanning the dark sky. Lucrécia's immobilized smile was passing through the clouds … My God, he mumbled gloomily. His stubborn head was needing to think about God in order to start thinking again. Fireflies were blinking, ironic, lighting up where he least expected them, encircling him like little devils.

But he didn't go back. He went ahead tough, a conqueror, heading toward the city that was the shelter of his strength. The closer he drew to the lights, the more he was vanquishing Lucrécia. Because this man, who would wipe his lips with his handkerchief, was made of stone. Whereas Lucrécia Neves wouldn't last long, Lucas knew it: she'd be substituted many times whereas he was whatever was permanent. She was so futile, so poor and obstinate. In fact five thousand lives wouldn't even be enough for her first real idea to reach perfection inside her. She'd already begun however the work of those five thousand lives.

The next day the doctor had hardly worked, awaiting the moment in which he'd see if the woman was still waiting for him in front of his office or if she'd disappeared. But with sudden horror and sudden joy—he found her. Standing, modest, smiling with her animal patience.

Their sleepwalking strolls began anew. And when late at night they stopped upon the hill, she said:

"Fortunately everything is impossible," and started scratching at the ground with the tip of her shoe. "Because I think I'd hurt the one I loved," she added gently and without pride, and those presumptuous words, so distant from her confused way of speaking, had come a long way before reaching this moment.

"What do I care how you'd hurt me," he said irritated.

She immediately halted her small kicks in the dirt.

Dazed, almost recoiling, she was wondering how it was possible for him to love her without knowing her, forgetting that she herself knew no more of the man than the love he was giving her.

Soon she was thinking quickly, seeking a way to show him the best of herself, to tell him about her life—with surprise she found nothing, turning over in vain the false pearls that seemed to have been her only jewels. In the urgency of the moment she remembered those nights in the living room … And though she rarely thought of them, and was hardly aware of their meaning—had they appeared to her as the only reality of her life? Eyes open in fright and watchfulness, she was tackling the memory of those nights that seemed to have been lost in her blood; forgetting was in fact her way of keeping something forever. In her affliction Lucrécia Neves was already wondering if she'd need to tell, what did it matter what form her days had taken? he too, everyone too seemed to be building around a forgotten thing … A delayed intelligence, having revealed the gesture to her, she thought she could describe it. But the moment of clairvoyance having passed, the lighthouse once again scanning other fields and leaving her in the dark—once again she wouldn't know the truth except by reliving even the useless moments. Oh, and she wouldn't even know how to use the necessary words.

Or did he understand. Because the doctor had spoken of São Geraldo in a tone that sometimes seemed stolen from her, and occasionally would say a word he only could have uttered if he knew what she knew … But if all that had happened without in fact Lucas's knowing the world in which she'd lived, and the words he'd uttered, identical to hers, had belonged to his own world …—then how many endless sets could form indefinitely with whatever was "there"? though one as much as the other, for different reasons, had severely cut their freedom.

Now resigned, scratching at the dirt once again, it also seemed to her pointless to talk. Because all of a sudden on the hill beside him, calm love seemed to be pointing out all things like the gesture. Ever since she started loving him she'd found simply the sign of fate she'd sought for so long, that irreplaceable substance that you barely suspected in things, the irreplaceableness of death: like the gesture, love was being reduced until reaching the irreplaceable, with love you could point out the world. She was lost.

"Let's stay friends," said the man who also didn't know how to speak and who for that reason needed to be forgiven.

"Friends?" mumbled the woman in soft surprise, "but we were never friends"—she breathed with pleasure—"we're enemies, my love, forever."

The doctor was suffering from the woman's inflexibility. Two previous generations had been lost in dead courtesy; it was painful to let blood open a new path through dry veins; he was suffering as much as he could.

But Lucrécia seemed calm. The doctor looked at her: she was sweet and cruel. Her canines were appearing in an innocent smile of rapture. And the man seemed to see for the first time the face of voluptuousness and patience. How could she be so mean, he thought with repugnance. But she's crazy, he was astonished shivering before the woman's joy: so she'd had the courage to lose herself to that extent. One day Lucrécia had said that, looking at the back of someone's neck, she'd sometimes be enraged.

The man wrinkled his eyebrows at this memory, joining it now to the sight of those sharp and happy teeth ... from what perverse past had she emerged. To see her in her childish perdition made him inhale with delight, in blind freedom. And that freedom was so rich that its excess was kindness; he enveloped her with his gaze, a wing that might cover her nudity—as it had so often before covered a dead person's shameless body. She didn't even notice him. But, anonymous like guardian angels, he was protecting that woman's joy.

That night Lucrécia didn't want him to walk her home and stayed on the hill alone.

It was dark but the constellations were blinking wet. Standing, as if on the only spot from which that view could be had, Lucrécia was looking at the darkness of the earth and of the sky. That movement infinitely spherical, harmonious and great: the world was round. Nun or murderess, she was discovering for a moment the nudity of her spirit. Nude, covered in fault as in forgiveness—and that's where the world was becoming the threshold of a leap. The world was the orb.

She was stroking her ear with her shoulder, cleaning herself. Sometimes she would peer into the dark with slight glances. The body so miserable. So proud. And everything so perishable. The trees planted all around. The wind low. It was intolerable. And precisely she was keeping this all in place. Why she precisely? each person she was seeing was precisely the person she was seeing. So many privileges.

The little woman's face looked scratched by the claws of a bird—could this be her expression of love. She'd reached a moment in which she didn't have the slightest freedom of action. Contradictorily in this instant when she'd act without any possible choice is when she'd become responsible. It even seemed to her, with impartiality and fairness, that she'd only sinned when it became impossible not to sin. Which wasn't making her faint of heart. She was as impassive as if she were the one who had scratched her face forever with the claws of an eagle. Even flapping, before fleeing, the dark wing against her cheek—with that hilarity that things contain before shining...

So this was love for people, she recognized. This love too was bright and inexplicable. But good—bread and wine and kindness. Yes, yes, she was quite lost. Though it had always seemed to her that first and foremost you had to get lost. She was well aware that, trying through the living room to look at the things that exist, she'd lacked the courage to be led by the objects: she'd fallen, yes, but had been afraid and clung to whatever she could. If she'd fallen all the way to the end, would she know what end of the fall it was to be under the starry sky? and to see that the world is round, and that the void is the plenitude, and that corn growing is spirit.

The whistle of the night ferry came from the sea, just more pained than that of a locomotive. The little woman bent over and stayed like that, laughing like a fool, ancient, with an almost recognizable demeanor. She herself recognizing the earth at last? marking it with her fleeting hoof like the fleeting place of life and death. Which was more than the imagination could aspire to.

The following night Lucas was the one who was waiting for her, and Lucrécia set out slowly, smiling.

Lucas no longer feared her face. And, in this moment in which they looked at each other naked, they saw without fright that in their nakedness he was a king and she a queen. Soon the darkness dotted with lights was enveloping them, the two were walking. Near a willow, for the thousandth time, for the first time, the doctor said: why didn't we know each other before? though they had known each other before. Passing through the thicket and giving him a kick, for the first time, for the thousandth time, aspiring to a rite, she wanted to die with him. Ah, to die of love, she said, wicked, leaning against the stone eagle. Looking at her, that was how Lucas saw her and remembered her later: humble, guarded by stone eagles.

And now they were calm looking at the hills.

Everything that would be impossible had taken the final form of mountains in the distance, and a delicateness of curves. While Lucas was staring at the already-erased horizon, Lucrécia started to examine him with such sweetness that she forgot herself. She was seeking in that face, where a singular perfection was transcending the obvious imperfection — seeking a spot through which to breach it. Which was making her feel so bad and so good as if seeking within herself the final resistance. The first light of the lighthouse revealed him nicely every once in a while but would blind the finer details of his face. Only in the dark would she see him.

Each feature would present separately a judgmental impersonality. In none of them did Lucrécia Neves find the love that she was giving him. Eventually she no longer would know what she was seeking, she was moving ahead held back only by the vertigo of a face.

It was between his mouth and nose — not in that space but in a possibility of selfish and blameless movement that could be sensed there, in that part that didn't even have a name — that she discovered where she loved him and where Lucas could be wounded. She imagined how much blood would spurt from that spot if through it the man were struck. And she saw, with a shock of pain and rapture, that a creature was only murderable in its beauty. She herself wounded by the chisel.

Impossible love piercing her with joy, she who belonged to

a man as she had belonged to things—wounded in the trunk of her species, standing, jubilant, rigid … Feeling on the surface of her skin thick horse veins. And Lucas, turning around to look at her: seeing her standing, isolated, in her equestrian grace. They finally touched.

In the morning Lucrécia Correia shut the house and crossed the gangplank over the mud. Birds in fast flight were making the water throw sparks. The sweetish smell of the dirty ferryboat at sea. And so many sunlit people, sitting with packages. The wind was batting their hair, the land far from view. Then an old man spat on the floor and there was the light gleaming on the floor: everyone was looking, empty with brightness. Lucrécia couldn't open her eyes without the day's striking them as blind lakes. Sitting in the bow with her parcels on her lap.

11   The First Deserters

PERSEU HAD TAKEN SHELTER FROM THE RAIN IN THE waiting room of the station, placing his suitcase on the bench. The day before he'd cut his hair. On his more naked face his ears seemed separate from his head; his slightly bony cheeks were making him look stubbornly weak and, despite this, tranquil.

His appearance had changed considerably since the days when he went out with Lucrécia. He was much thinner, less handsome. Now he had a way of being sweet that no longer resided in sweetness; with the raincoat loose on his body he looked like a foreigner who was entering a city.

It was raining a lot. The rain on the still-deserted tracks had a clandestine meaning to which he seemed to belong.

Since he had time, he turned on the radio that was soon popping picking up the distant storm—the thread of music however could be detected through the crackling of electricity. Perseu was listening while standing, without dreams and without anything you might call understanding. The musical phrase, very noble, was as visible to him as the radio. He was grasping the effort of the music with the same agreeable effort, and taking pleasure in this vague rivalry. When people would ask him if he liked music, he'd say smiling charmingly that he liked it well enough, but didn't understand it, hearing a knock at the door amounted to almost the same thing as hearing music.

The radio was crackling. Perseu was listening with peaceful strength, stroking the paperweight on the small table. If he'd lived in his own time he'd be tempted to think that the music was making him suffer. But this insignificant young man hadn't had real influences or left any mark. Maybe he really was out of step with his time, and so much freedom was making him fall short of what he could have done if he'd been held back. But he always seemed to get by in silence. If he didn't understand the obscure notes, he was following them with a small enigmatic part of himself that was enjoying itself inside the clarity of the mystery. When the music ceased, he turned off the radio. The raindrops were falling from the gutters and the jug that the station manager had left outside was filling with water.

Perseu was resting standing up. He was tired and tranquil. Near his mouth two slight descending lines were foreshadowing a man's wrinkles. Since he wasn't particularly of his time, which would have made him suffer, nor had a culture from which to pick out feelings—he was standing, caressing the glass paperweight, with the two wrinkles taking shape: intact, pensive, a bit fatigued. Without being a father, he was already no longer a son. He found himself at a luminous and neutral point. And he wouldn't transmit this reality to anyone. Especially not to any woman. As he'd never give his harmony or the shape of his body. He could pacify a woman. But his strange peace, he wouldn't communicate.

The station bell was announcing the departure. Perseu

entered the compartment, placed his suitcase under the seat. When the train left, he swayed happily looking side to side.

Soon they were leaving the metropolitan area and entering the countryside. It kept raining, the soaked land looking sad with such dark trees. Within the sleeping noise of the wheels and of the rainy wind, the car was proceeding calmly at this end of the afternoon. Perseu had drunk two glasses of port so as not to catch cold since he was still meticulous about his health and exercise. With the alcohol in his heart he was feeling a bit too good, almost anxious. He was applying his uneasiness to concrete things: looking at every object of the coach lending them somber contentment.

In the compartment each person had a face, extremely visible in the transmuted afternoon light. A face was like a name, he thought with pleasure and disquiet. His thought was just the rhythm of the wheels. Perseu had no more than the shape for an extraordinary thought, and not the thought, and that was exciting him — face is one thing, body something else, wine in the body something else. Though he felt fully complete with his raincoat in a train.

He began by looking at a common girl, with large features. "She looks like a flower," he thought agitated. She had round eyes. Empty because she was alone. You couldn't say if they were happy, thoughtful or alert — merely physical eyes, and someone might doubt they could see. Yet her eyelids were blinking with sparse lashes and eating the air with delicacy. Suddenly Perseu started to like them with stubbornness and pleasure. They were perched above a large nose that was breathing with effort: the girl had a cold, and was slightly opening her thick lips. The whole face was exterior, a flower to be taken. Desire even came to him. The type of heavy head you might grasp with both hands and look at with useless sincerity—before you knew it thinking about some other thing, except with that tedious object in your hands, because it would be impossible to concentrate on that corolla face. He began to imagine how hard it would be to get to know her because she'd lie—as soon as she was touched, she'd close up completely in lies and dreams, she'd get "interesting," say she had so many suitors, her family so well-off, she thank God in good health, and even how she was a virgin—Perseu had a murmur of satisfaction seeing how far his experience had reached and imagining himself pretending to believe her, kissing her while she lied—which would be very indecent and very tender.

Meanwhile she showed that she'd foreseen the young man: she seemed to think faster and, almost without transforming her immaculate face, had become interesting: Perseu averted his gaze.

It seemed to him immodest to attract attention. That however was what always happened to him. His calm insignificance would make people lift their eyes and stare at him inquisitively, which was strangely mixed with a bit of insolence. Which would bother him. But most of the time he was noticed only unconsciously, the way you look at the day. In fact the silent couple looked at him quickly, in no time, as if he were the only passenger. The flushed woman had a sensitive chin and small eyes. The man was weak, disoriented: his face shaved and greenish, green eyes, ashen and well-made hands.

"The cattle."

The train was running warm in the rain.

"Alfredo, the cattle," said the woman in a hoarse voice.

Perseu stared at a dusty corner of the floor and then at the suitcase belonging to a woman in black—with his mouth full of saliva, the thickest vein in his heart having burst, he had the first painful feeling of passion and mercy.

"People," he thought feeling ashamed. In the fields the wet cows were hot, sluggish. "Folks," he said. A sensibility within him was becoming a man. And that would be his most interior life.

With the fact of being a man he wanted to look at the world, and saw the fields in the rain, the worn front steps of a house. The people were tepid on the train, the smoke comforting. He was looking at everything with innocence, power and dominion.

The lady in black was smoking, examining him with painted eyes. Perseu didn't like women on whom nothing was lost. But he experienced a certain hot promise in his chest upon seeing a perfumed and clever woman observing him. Though that direct gaze intimidated him. That bold gaze?

But no.

Right then the woman in black was thinking while exhaling smoke: there all of a sudden is a man. Which was amazing to her. But it was late for her. There all of a sudden is a man, she guessed and, putting out her cigarette, addressed the discovery, in defiance—through the ever-growing distance—in defiance and compassion to a person who during their short separation wouldn't know what to do with himself.

Perseu however was no longer looking at her, interested now in penetrating the darkness through the window. No woman would receive the heat of his soul that he might one day give to a friend. He'd forgotten the woman and was peering at the night through the window—unstable, big, silent in his raincoat. But he wasn't just a blind force. Being a man was leading him through the mystery.

He sat with the lady in black at the station bar. She ordered a drink, took out a cigarette. No, thank you, he didn't smoke. Hearing that answer she seemed even more ironic, despite wrapping him in a broad gaze that made him uncomfortable. He didn't like women with such big eyes. Right at the exit of the train she'd asked him to help carry her suitcase to the restaurant. Surprised, Perseu had walked ahead of her, placed the suitcase next to a table and bowed a bit rigidly bidding farewell. But the woman, who didn't stop staring at him calmly, had invited him to drink something before they both headed into the city.

The small room was poorly lit by shaded lamps on the only three tables. Perseu's brief interest in the woman had gone out, leaving just his impatience to go his own way.

Being thus abducted vaguely reminded him of someone. And, looking at that creature, did the young man anxiously feel that the same race was stalking him? he wondered whether Lucrécia Neves might now have that woman's face. In fact the weak light of the bar was straining his eyes. And in the filthy brightness, the increasingly unknown creature before him was flickering a fantastical face. Perseu's complacent nature wouldn't let him admit that the woman was simply annoying him, those enormous eyes, her constant smoke and the determination with which she'd grabbed him … Old and cynical, he thought without rage, with a certain sympathy. She was smoking and drinking, and wasn't looking at him much now. A vague concept of chivalry was keeping him from excusing himself; he was waiting for the woman to decide to get up.

But she seemed to have time. Though she wouldn't release him, she'd sometimes forget him—she'd lean over the table, hold her glass with one hand, stroke it with the other, peering at the liquid in slightly ardent meditation. It was raining harder and making the wooden gangplank outside tremble. Perseu kept trying to chat but she wasn't giving him any encouragement. He was putting up with the nuisance of the situation only because in this unfamiliar scene others might see an adventure: so he was examining his companion, trying to guess what category she'd fall into.

Despite being friendly to all women, he divided them into the ones who were worthwhile and the ones who weren't. What made it hard to find anything to discuss was that she was so much older than he was.

Yet the woman would know where the young man's awkwardness was coming from, and even how to dispel it; her understanding had sharpened to the point of shamelessness. But in fact she wasn't worried about what the skinny young man might think. What she herself was really worried about, she couldn't say. She just knew that, in ferocity, she was clinging to this moment, and this was already the fourth glass she was drinking in order to keep the young man. Meanwhile the possibility of hilarity became intolerable when the young man asked:

"Are you married, ma'am?"

She was rigid, and telling herself: I could be his mother. Which wasn't true, she'd thought it to wound herself. She might even scream if he got up—that was all she knew.

What did she want anyway from this beautiful young man? he was clearly bored … But that wouldn't stop her; things were now running along so fast that they were making her serious, ferocious, her hands stiffening on the tablecloth. If she wanted to be upfront and lay her cards on the table, she wouldn't have any cards—that's how far she'd gone.

Here all of a sudden is a man, she was thinking. Men had always seemed excessively beautiful to her—that's what she'd felt when centuries ago, in her parents' house, in a ball gown, she'd resembled a young tree with few leaves—the memory had made her terribly ironic later.

And you couldn't tell why the weak had later become her prey. Then, when she'd meet a weak and intelligent man, above all weak because intelligent—she'd devour him roughly, not let him find his balance, make him need her forever—that's what she'd do, absorbing them, detesting them, supporting them, the ironic mother. Her power had become great. When a defeated person would approach—she'd understand that person, she'd understand; how well you understand me, Afonso said. An object had always needed to be flawed in order for her to be able to seize it, and through its flaw. She'd buy it cheaper, that way.

What did she want now from this young man? a little excited by the drink, she was saying to herself: just look how ridiculous I've become. Also he was unusual. I don't want to understand him, she was repeating sensitive to the cold, aged. Because, a moment more, and she'd understand him so well that she'd weaken this "marvelous" person before her, who— ah, "a marvel"—didn't need anyone.

Oh, but to understand him for a minute. And he, already no longer unassailable, would need her. The same young man from the first dances, the same angel who'd asked her to dance and who'd disappeared in order to be an engineer … It was also her own mother whom she, the daughter, could only reach after learning her sins—increasing their gravity in order to be able to love better.

She could also only summon this distracted perfection before her by destroying it through understanding.

But would he be distracted? or was she the one who wasn't there. She'd certainly noted on the train that the young man seemed remote from the passengers. Maybe just because he'd been present and was real. The others were the ones who had moved off and were seeing him from afar. She'd made him out when she'd said in surprise: here suddenly is a man.

This was someone who didn't want or need to flee: he was going, and wherever he'd go she'd go too. She too had already lived through this time. But what had remained of the simple richness in her first ball gown? what had survived of her undefined and professionless intelligence that "marveled"—the word that had become her own, always changing meaning, "a marvel," spoken by so many of her voices, one loud at the height of an event—a marvel—another full, cavernous, tremulous—a marvel—another down there, quick like a stream—a marvel. What had happened to the audacity of being weak? she hadn't dared to be. And to the mirror where she'd looked at herself for a second? the fruit gnawed by a worm, the "marvel" with the dark larva in its heart.

She quickly smiled at the young man, time was pressing, there wasn't a minute to lose. The young man smiled back. Unable not to notice, she discovered in that answer a certain artificial and uncomfortable immorality: out of friendliness he was giving whatever a tired woman's face was seeming to request. But she leapt over this too—never to be held back now by an obstacle—leapt over, kept running in search of the whole fruit, the gold of the fruit on the tree, the ball gown, the big eyes in the mirror, that beginning of understanding that was just the world around her, and which had later become her weapon, her image before putting the cape on her shoulders and leaving—the golden fruit in the mirror—a marvel!

she too had once been incomprehensible, remote! I never saw such big eyes, said in the lights a young man in black.

With a start Perseu and the woman heard the deaf noise of an airplane above the station. The hoarse wings further darkened the small room filling it with somber luxury. The airplane went off and the city was pulsing in silence.

Again the air of the room awoke blinking in the lamps—the toothpick holder on the tablecloth: the whole thing was sordid, Perseu was saying to himself protecting himself.

And "marvelous," the woman was saying. The transformations of the bar were the monotonous mutations of an insomnia, the watchfulness of the lady in black stretching out in shadow, her eyelashes flapping somnolent over the black luminosity of her eyes. The fruit was wavering full. As in a children's game in the garden, she was supposed to seize it with her mouth, no hands—anyway she'd never had hands— and since she didn't have hands she'd reminded Perseu of that decapitated body that had belonged to Lucrécia. She was supposed to seize it with her own disturbance, with the darkness that was still her only strength, the darkness full of honeybees. But first she'd have to give up forever, first lay down her weapon—be only the dark stain in the mirror—and there the fruit would be. First, turn away the thing that had been her conquest until reaching the universal and dreamy attention of a dog—and behold, behold the whole fruit. For hadn't that been the way she'd seen herself in the mirror?

Afterward much time had passed, she'd learned a loud way of speaking with children, saying funny phrases for the benefit of the adults around her; only the children wouldn't get it. They were whole. Remote like the young man. But if the lady in black saw a dog—a real dog—even today she'd still know how to reach it, which proved that the "marvel" kept wavering. She knew like nobody else how to transform a solitary dog into a happy dog that would lie at her side blinking his eyes. And then, with him at her feet—never, never comprehensible—the room would grow large, silent; and it wasn't the dog, she was the one who was guarding the house. Such was her greatness, such her misery.

The young man across from her was a big dog, skinny, solitary. Not to be able to be him, how unfair. With the same center of somber purity. With the soul that dogs have: belonging to the house, to steps, corner of the yard; with that gaze over the world that a stretched-out dog has. The lady in black thought about her wrinkles—there wasn't an instant in which they weren't getting deeper, there wasn't a minute to lose, she kept running, jumping over streams, sensing the direction of the wind, leaping in the darkness in search of the moment in the forest in which she'd say: a marvel.

The dusty toothpick holder on the tablecloth. Perseu was fighting off Lucrécia's ghost, and this woman who, coming certainly from a great urban center, was repeating the mystery of bad women. The young man's face had covered itself in shadows, his eyes shining from a distant and tranquil depth.

Whatever was tranquil was even more distant, whatever was perfect was becoming remoter yet—for the girl on the night of the dance everything was impossible. How beautiful he is, she thought. Here suddenly is a person. She was so maternal that it was horrible. She was seeing the young man's hands, the pungent cleanliness of his nails, the dark tie. Never—the young man's polite face was saying. Never—the neck supporting his hard and perfect head was repeating. It was a bit terrible. Not just to her was spoken in him "never"—"never" was spoken much more gravely on his forehead without wrinkles, on that delicate mouth.

But she wasn't afraid. It was "not forgetting later" that was scaring her: she wouldn't be able to stand surviving. And she was already calming down: let the young man pass without destroying her way of lighting her cigarette, her high voice, all this was her peace. She didn't want him to make her lose her way of dealing with whatever had been left behind and abandoned after the train had departed, nor lose the tranquility of showing him her cards—all this was a construction. The peace of taking the train knowing with calm that in the other city there awaiting her would be a hotel room and a balcony from which she could look out before going to sleep; she was the owner of this desert where on the balcony she was smoking a cigarette. She wasn't ashamed not to want a new life—a new life was very dangerous, who among you could stand it. The lady in black put out her cigarette.

During this interval, the perfect being had a leg that had fallen asleep and was discreetly trying to wake it. Good that he didn't have to explain where he'd been all this time. What for, where was he anyway? There was no room under the table to stretch his leg, and the numbness was giving his face a stubborn expression. He was imagining, as in an impossible dream, getting up, unfolding his wings and shaking himself until recovering his sleeping virility.

Seeing that woman who was smoking and drinking, the young man had in his sleepwalking the desire to draw her close at last, or to touch her with his knee under the table; it was a slightly cruel and dreamy desire, from which he would easily refrain. With a woman like that it seemed to him he needed above all else to know how to talk, say interesting things. He'd never know if she were expecting a statement about life from him, about the vain passage of the things of this world. That's how, in his foolishness, he'd imagined Lucrécia Neves, and he wanted to apply the experience to his new companion.

He observed, without moreover blaming himself, not being one of those brilliant men, able to please a woman by telling her what she wants to hear. He reflected with moroseness that despite not constantly thinking "about sexual matters" he must have been loutish since with a woman he'd draw discussions to a close and embrace her with some strength. Friendships with women displeased him—the idea would make him smile intimidated like the idea of entering a women's bathroom.

And now, because he glanced at her for an instant and because their eyes met—both of them had been waiting for years.

Amidst the fatigue of both there was a moment of impatience, almost of rage, in which the room became darker and more intense as if a train were about to leave; irate, the two focused on the toothpick holder, on the lamp, on everything that was small and lost, so refined that they'd irritate an onlooker. Even now, without losing the habit of calming people, he smiled at her.

Which frightened her: was the young man trying to take his leave? not yet! she thought, and if she'd spoken she would have been hoarse. The drink and the rain, and the somber arousal, and the marvel before her—and she greedy … He too was drinking, resigned to losing a few more minutes with that old lady, chivalrous, horribly polite like the others, yes, yes, let's dance—she was rushing, smoking her cigarette down to the butt almost burning her nails …

"… what's your name."

"Perseu," he said surprised waking up.

"Perseu!" she repeated with a shock on the verge of laughter. How idiotic, with a name like that. She guessed smiling that he came from some township where important names were common. Perseu.

And maybe because of the absurdity of the name, because of the notion of time that was passing, because of the beauty of the name—she grew very tired. The little empty room, a train passing through the station, the suitcases. Everything grew dark, the scene transported itself into sleep—everything had become obscured intimately, inside the drink. And in the shadow the gentle heart of the woman, without pain, in fatigued love. I'm yours, she thought lying, a bit nauseated. The weak lamp was keeping its balance in the station, it was very nice to live but she needed to throw up. Everything was heavy. Drops of rain were streaming. The young man irremovable … could he be winking at her? she winked back at him—finally in the center of this small world, in this comforting disorder of life, with queasiness, black eyes full of gold. What a marvel.

It lasted only a moment, like some spark, and was threatening; intimate and threatening. Behold, behold the "truth." That's how at a mature age you had to call the "marvel."

She got up, disappeared through a door. Perseu terrorized heard her throwing up. Before long she was coming back wiping her mouth, her eyes even bigger, and smiling delighted with modesty. A train approached shaking the little room.

The woman was smiling entirely inside herself, with a certain boredom. I think I can let him go now, she thought. At first she'd clung with her split nails to each minute. But now she was distended as after an operation and wanted to be alone with her bandages.

She examined one more time the young man she, with so

much effort, had left intact—looked at him and shook her head like an old lady. She would have liked to push two chairs together, curl up and sleep. She was still feeling grateful to some thing, and her voice, when she coughed, came out husky. So thankful to the boy who'd let her, maybe a little too late—between a train and a hotel, without even abandoning her suitcase—who'd let her simply admire him; she who was always demanding that people suffer, otherwise where could she start to gnaw them? and especially where to forgive them.

Wanting nothing now from the young man, liking him with benevolence and distraction; without trying to steal anything from him; sleepy, fighting back tears that preceded a yawn, thinking with mechanical pleasure about snuggling with "that other one" who was in the distant city nervously awaiting a telegram, that one from whom she'd be separated for a week—which was so much, which was so little.

"Perseu," she said urbanely, savoring with humorous intelligence whatever was ridiculous and charming in his name, "Perseu, I have to go now and so do you."

The young man awoke, smiled with sleep—another instant and the dark light of the room would let them walk in slow leaps; a moment more they'd fall asleep face down on the table, to the sound of the rain. Waking up he started to search his pocket. She removed without haste the money from her purse and placed it on the tablecloth. Perseu tried to object but, since she said nothing, gave in. Both seemed to find it natural for the woman to pay. After all she was the one who'd ordered. It's the least that could happen to me, she thought sleepily, without irony.

Perseu put her suitcase in a taxi, she got in. Seated, already comfortable, she hesitated a bit, and ended up offering him a ride; he refused ceremoniously, she lightly sighed with relief. When the young man shut the door, however, the woman felt some remorse seeing him standing in the light of the streetlamp, in the rain: tall with his raincoat, pleasant. Very pleasant, she thought. So easy to find with him some common ground, with that short hair … Some remorse and a franker camaraderie — and also surprise: because under the streetlamp, friendly, skinny, was the same perfect being she'd spared, the marvel. A certain duty too, habit more than anything else: it wasn't hard to understand him somewhat, give him a bit, not too much. She brought her head closer to the window, smiled with command, with a somewhat professional appearance that was momentarily removing the age from her face:

"You're a student …"

"No, a doctor," he said lowering himself to the height of the window and looking at her with distrust.

"That's what I thought …"—He too smiled, his attention awakened. She suddenly seemed like a friend, and this was removing her danger as a woman. He smiled more and without noticing was grasping the handle of the door delaying the car's departure. The enemy from the bar had disappeared.

"You're working, Perseu."

"I am, I'm starting out at the hospital here."

"Ah, so you work at a hospital."—The two looked at each other. She in a social situation, he on the lookout.—"Look, Perseu, I'm sure you'll be a good doctor."—He faced her suspicious.—"The kind you call even when you're healthy, just to be sure you're really alive," she smiled wittily.

Yes, he hoped so, he answered bending over more, smiling.

Maybe she …; but no. Yes, maybe? … anyway what could she do? Foolishness. But she was no longer a stranger. And that same look you could find in the friend you awaited without impatience ... The lady in black was giving the address to the driver, and saying from the back of the car, where Perseu could no longer see her intelligent and disturbing face, and once again with the same voice from the bar:

"Thanks for everything."

The car drove off. He remained standing on the sidewalk.

Since the rain was getting worse he adjusted his cloak and finally crossed the deserted flagstones. He'd be a good doctor, she'd said it with such assurance. "It's because there are things you can see right away," he thought, happy.

Could it have been the woman's words that were giving him a slightly stifling hope? and also disgust. He was well aware that certain things, even good things, should never be touched, not even with thought. He never spoke of the already slightly anxious certainty that he'd become a good doctor. Giving him the hope of being a good doctor, the woman hadn't allowed him anything more ... Yet if he himself should talk, he'd say that this was his desire. But he simply didn't talk, that's the difference. A little bitterness. Tired; the perfect being for an instant struck.

I'm of the opinion that people talk too much, he thought stubbornly.

But his strength was greater than that of a word spoken by a disturbed woman. Soon, walking in the wet streets, he was recovering the vague right born in the train and that even if nebulous was enough; he'd reacquire the peace of a man from before the accidents, not sharing his hope, and above all not talking; people talk too much. He turned up his collar seeking the house numbers in the weak light.

Neither Lucrécia Neves's innocence, nor the damnation of the woman in black, neither of these avid female beings who'd fade in the presence of reality could touch him because he was reality: a silent young man tucked into a raincoat. That's how they'd see him from a window, the curious hand drawing back the curtain; and he was no more than that. Avoiding the puddles. Moreover he was free: he wasn't asking for proof.

He walked looking at the buildings in the rain, impersonal and omniscient again, blind in the blind city; but an animal knows its forest; and even if it gets lost—getting lost is a path too.

12   *End of the Construction: The Viaduct*

IN THE LAST DAYS OF HIS LIFE MATEUS CORREIA HAD seemed abashed in the face of the gravity of what was happening to him and even irritated as if he didn't deserve so much. The closer a certain hour approached, the more he smiled with modesty at his wife, in a sorrow that until then certainly hadn't had the chance to show itself. Though the minute before dying could have, because of its urgency, lasted long enough to give him time to have been absolutely happy, like a crystal.

His face seemed proud. What would such an inexperienced soul do without the solution that the body had been. Lucrécia was crying shocked.

And now alone, she'd sit at night listening to the silence of Market Street.

Some thing kept working noiselessly, she in the prow of the ship—down below the machines functioning almost without a sound. For a moment she'd see Mateus again. And in a slap to the face, maybe he hadn't even had wide hips! he'd just been pale, with a mustache.

Dying of a heart attack had come to explain that thick calm and choosing so many dishes: okay then, I'm going to see a little star. Mateus had gone to see a little star—which made her start crying again.

Why hadn't she seen him in the loveliest way to be seen? He'd been good like every man who'd end up dying, and she'd loved him. She just hadn't understood in time that ordering the sink pipes to be cleaned or lunching with the whole weight of his body—was his form of joy. What had she wanted from him? the widow was blaming herself: that he apply his joy to flowers, as in the Association? No, when he'd embraced her and she'd been good to him, Mateus would say: if the sink breaks again the one who'll pay next time is the plumber. Even his death, she'd tried to destroy. She'd tried to console him, the only way of reducing the event to something recognizable: at least you're not dying in someone else's house. But this the man hadn't allowed; without speaking he'd looked at her smiling with embarrassment: you fool, as if dying weren't always in someone else's house. Oh, if she could see him again and give him her best gaze, not even that: she'd give him what her husband had hoped for from her, her humble life and not desires. The widow was weeping full of regret.

Forgetting him more and more.

To tell the truth she'd only remember Mateus objectively when she'd see him again in his coughing fits, which were almost silent from so much violence without escape: he'd cough shaking the house in silence. Or when her husband would appear in her dreams. Smiling, good as the root of his life had been: oh, she hadn't understood that each person was the utmost and there was no need to seek another: that's how she was trying to think in order for Mateus to hear, and in her dreams he would hear her. As always, without understanding very well.

So she wrote to Ana: "Mother dear, Mateus passed away, only another woman can understand a widow's despair! Yet I think that"…

While writing she was relying more and more on connective words, on various "howevers" and "thens," buying herself time. Because it was enough to have to express herself, and the stubborn woman would fall mute, and almost have to create some feeling to say. She lifted her head biting the tip of her pencil: the sun was disappearing red and hot, each object was keeping itself within a golden thread. And in the door the key as lit up as the horizon—Lucrécia was pushing her hair away from her fatigued forehead. Atop the vanity the perfumes were trembling in their bottles: "only another woman can understand," she finished.

Then the house brightened, the windows opened, and everything, washed by tears, was going well, her health now stable.

In the streets, then, people were moving in scattered light and without effort; whatever had been mortal had been reached, and the rest was eternal, without danger. Once again Lucrécia Neves's life was opening with a certain majesty, doors slamming, that brightness of air that has no name, the house again full of material security: such were her bright days of widowhood, the trinket playing the flute.

When she'd go out she was shocked by São Geraldo's leap of progress, terrified in the traffic like a hen who'd fled the yard. The streets no longer smelled of the stable but of a weapon fired—steel and gunpowder.

And how the tires would explode! Countless offices had been opened with typewriters, installations of iron filing cabinets and automatic pens. Copies and copies were typed out in mimeographs and signed. The filing cabinets were bursting, full of the immediate registry of whatever was going on. The men from Municipal Hygiene were superficially sweeping the sidewalks, hiding the debris in the gutters. Which in the afternoon would sparkle in the final rays of sunlight in dust and luster, like treasures.

The widow too had been transformed. These days her face was weak and bore measured expressions. If she'd fought her habit of lowering the corners of her mouth, now she'd let herself go, and this gesture had given her an even more impersonal way of facing things. When she went to the dentist and put in two gold teeth—she finally had her first foreign look.

She also noticed that by opening her eyes wide she'd look younger. So she'd open her eyes in continual astonishment, which accentuated her appearance of an outsider passing through. If she didn't gain youthfulness, she reached some beauty of form, so that if she could be regarded as an object, she'd be thought pretty. But if seen as someone who could speak ...—nobody had time to see her in any way at all.

Which didn't stop her: she'd take tea with astonished eyes above the teacup, ready to be photographed. Suddenly—the snapshot taken—moving on, picking up a cookie with her fingertips: what a perfect afternoon, thought Lucrécia Neves Correia looking out from the new confectionery on Market Street, now Silva Torres Avenue.

Next she'd head to the garden with her reading under her arm: the pamphlet "Spiritual Cancer." She'd hardly descended the steps of the park, and was whirled by her eyes—how many weeds had been torn out! how many weeds coming up, how much order, young children whose parents she didn't know—and what a sun, how hard to climb, so easy to find things lost on the ground, in the spoils of the old São Geraldo—she found a patron saint prayer card—so easy to find what others had lost but never, never finding what lost itself: that's what she thought and opened the pamphlet to the first chapter: "Cursing Is Cancer Too." She was trying to be dignified with elevated thoughts. And, if she didn't find any, at least she was nodding her head, outraged by the baseness of our day and age.

That day she saw two boys fighting. The young fighters were striking each other in the face, white with anger and silence. Because it was so intense, the scene had lost its sonority. Only a little bird was singing in the tree above. The widow was blanching with horror. An older man separated them and said if they kept fighting he'd pull them by the ears. Which, even to Lucrécia, sounded strange: in São Geraldo children's ears were no longer being pulled. The boys stopped, looked at him in silence. One was cross-eyed. The little bird was singing. One of the kids finally spat on the ground in defiance and fled jeering him … the other ran, looking back and laughing. They were enemies but were uniting against the great common adversary, in this case, that man from another time who embarrassed was looking at Lucrécia.

She, still a bit undone, smiled at him. He said: excuse me, ma'am, and sat respectfully on her bench. Happy to be together, they made themselves comfortable and chatted about kids nowadays. He pleasantly surprised to find her so sensible despite being young, without knowing that São Geraldo had been the one that left her behind. And she beside him able to look with another assurance at the new monument to the Union of Posts and Telegraphs.

Returning home in a better mood, sitting down to knit on the back terrace; looking at the dark rooftops and the factory towers, dry extremities of the world. They weren't mature like the living room where small pieces of furniture, pitchers, shadows, trinkets were piling up; merely renewed by another day that might bring a new position to the things. Looking at the towers of the power plants with serene eyes, satisfied. For having been in spite of everything prudent, warding off illnesses, avoiding the greater danger of things, keeping with care whatever was hers—this being the only explanation she'd found to justify her passion for the house and the trinkets: "so then! you'd kept with care whatever was yours!" If seeing the way she'd spared herself made her nervous with a certain shame, the answer would occur to her: yes, but there she was. Finally seated. She interrupted her knitting, inhaled with sweet ardor.

The house too had managed to reach the present moment. Old, low, full of the broad and virginal chorus of that afternoon. The woman was peering with pleasure at a smokestack that the air was surrounding with insistent brightness. If she'd lost the reason for her habits, she still kept them and, if she'd forgotten the true turning toward the living room, she kept her way of looking at the room—which filled her days with surveillances without explanations, with small interrupted beginnings between clearings of her throat and useless rushing. Meeting her "commitment" was no longer creating it. It was inquiring whether in the life lived some thing had been fulfilled.

And indeed, it had been. It was a very difficult thought to see that indeed it had been. Oh, nothing important, just irreplaceable. It had been fulfilled much more mutely: from object to object, a certain daily ascension always independent of thought, time moving ahead. In what moment and in the face of what object had she said, for example: "I am Lucrécia. My soul is immortal"—when?

Well, never. "But let's suppose I'd said it." That's how the woman felt she had to reason. Because from real life, lived day to day, there had remained for her—if she didn't want to lie—just the possibility of saying, in a conversation between neighbor women, in a mixture of long experience and last-minute discovery: yes, yes, the soul is important too, don't you think?

Telling her "story" was even harder than living it. If only because "living now" was just a car driving in the heat, some thing advancing day by day like whatever ripens, today it was the ship on the high seas.

She herself feeling the way others would call her by her name, and see her as a widow, and the way the fishmongers would scheme to sell her cheaper fish.

And some haughtiness. From being so patient, she'd finally reached a certain point, a dog barking far off, the hill in the pasture now accessible thanks to the viaduct, the gaze continuing to be her utmost reflection, and the proliferated things: scissors on the table, wings, cars constantly shaking the second floor that one day would be demolished, the shadow of airplanes over the city. At night the Southern Cross above the rooftops and the woman snoring tranquil, nautical.

Up to this moment when she was knitting on the terrace.

The luminous dust encircling her, happy machine that would function in quick silence. From the continuous movement of hands a spirit and an ease being born—and, without surprise, clairvoyance within clairvoyance like darkness within darkness: for this was the afternoon light.

As for her herself—aware, simply aware. For whom all this was insurmountable even by the imagination—that hard truth of sun and wind, and of a man walking, and of things set down. And a person didn't even know how to limit himself. For she couldn't even refrain from taking pride in seeing time pass—

but is it February already?—as if this development were her own. And it was. And Perseu had made her so fulfilled. And so often she "had said" because—over there was an open window. A person was Olympic.

A person was Olympic and empty. Seated with legs spread, hands crossed over her belly.

Oh, she'd lived from a story much greater than her own. How to limit yourself to your own story if right over there was the tower of the power plant? That truth made from being able to look. She'd never really thought; thinking would be simply inventing.

The corn growing in the field had been her greatest thought. And the horse was the beauty of man. That's how things were. Her peace had been the beauty of a horse. Could that be the story of an empty life?

Suddenly, in the middle of her knitting, just for glory, the woman standing up and beating somber wings over the finished city—somber as animals were somber, morose and free; somber without pain being suffering; whatever there'd been of the impersonal in her life was making her fly.

The afternoon had darkened and the widow took advantage of the dusk to curl up; in the silence they'd opened abundant water, so she leaned over in order to spot the bucket that the water was filling with a sound ever more level and singing, her heart curious like an old woman's. Sensitive, sensitive. Everything she'd had that was most precious was outside her: the water in the bucket? they'd poured it all on the dry lot of the store. From the soaked land was rising the suffocating smell of dust—the widow Correia faked a cough, just in order to express herself too.

She'd reached without any doubt a certain point of glory.

São Geraldo too had reached a certain point, ready to change its name, according to the newspapers. This was all that could be said anyway, this was all you could see, and she was seeing.

Her face had taken on an almost physical dignity, finally possible to be transmitted to a child—except this child would go through life trying to justify his inheritance, carrying blindly forward the obscure race of builders. Who possessed courage as a tradition.

It was a few days later that she received her mother's letter summoning her to the farm.

"There's a man here with a very good heart, my child, who saw your picture and liked it and always asks about you and your life, my dear girl. I tell him that you lead the life of a saint."

I don't understand! Lucrécia broke in startled—what did her photograph still want?

Spending days with the letter at her breast.

And finally making up her mind to sell the house and be reunited with her picture. Sighing with joy. The widow, the widow, she was saying laughing, teasing herself.

He's my second husband, she was shocking herself as if she had no right to so much luck. She only really had the right to Doctor Lucas, the woman was reflecting without explaining herself.

Ah, the widow, she broke in emotionally moved rereading the letter a thousand times. "There's a man here ...," she'd sing by heart. She'd look at the portrait hanging on the hallway wall in order to divine what was awaiting her, the merry widow. She'd end up laughing again. Oh, it was later and later.

Later and later it was. Serious, ardent, she ran to the living room, grabbed the cold trinket and touched it to her cheek, her eyes shut. So she'd abandon all this ...? On her big horse face the tear was running down. And the trinket built by her eyes ...

But she'd abandon it and abandon the mercantile city that the excessive pride in her destiny had raised, with an embankment and a viaduct, all the way to the slope of nameless horses.

The siege of São Geraldo had been lifted.

Henceforth it would have a history that would no longer interest anyone, left to its serious subdivisions, to its fines, to its stones and park benches, miserly as one whose treasures, as punishment, no one coveted any longer. Its defense system, now useless, remained standing in the sun, as a historical monument. Its inhabitants had deserted it or from it their spirits had deserted. Though they were also surrendered to freedom and to solitude.

If they had lowered the drawbridge, nonetheless along the Almeida Bastos Viaduct no one still thought to reach the old fortress, the hill.

From which the last horses had already emigrated, surrendering the metropolis to the glory of its mechanism.

Maybe—as Lucrécia Neves would say—one day São Geraldo would have underground rail lines. This seemed to be the abandoned city's only dream.

The widow hardly had time to pack up her things and escape.

BERN, MAY 1948.

Appendix: A Response to a Response

Shortly after The Besieged City *was published in 1949, Temístocles Linhares (1905–1993) published a review in a leading Rio newspaper. It is a good reflection of the perplexity many early readers felt in the face of Clarice Lispector's unprecedented style—and the break with novelistic tradition it represented.*

Twenty-two years later, Clarice happened upon the review and published a short reply in her weekly newspaper column.

THE SPELL OF THE PHRASE
(PUBLISHED IN *A MANHÃ*, OCTOBER 23, 1949)

When *Near to the Wild Heart* appeared, the native critics fell all over themselves. Mrs. Clarice Lispector was bringing a new contribution to novelistic technique, or rather, a flexibility to language by giving it another sense of inquiry and discovery that led to great expectations.

This contribution was all the more valued since it occurred

in an area where we'd hardly begun to crawl, the novel of inner life, where words are no longer simply signs or sounds but are transformed instead into ideal values or essential feelings.

What she was doing was really important and deserved warm praise. And that's why the critics didn't hold back, extending the honors due a person debuting in our literature with a quite original means of expression, able to capture many of the subtle and fleeting movements in our lives, occurrences that generally find no explanation.

It would be unfair not to mention, moreover, the abundant lyricism that ran through almost every scene of the book and had as its catalyzing element its central figure, that Joana, with something autobiographical about her, through whose mind images and already-felt emotions ran over and over, without modifying at all her irreducible personality, "hard, crystalline," when placed in contact with reality. Indeed, no matter what Joana did to try to identify with herself, what remained instead ended up being "knowledge for knowledge's sake." Her lyricism seemed to clash with the analytic spirit that denied her the possibility of communion or fusion with other worlds, so different from her own. Her own world may have had some privileged meaning and in her that meaning was reduced to a kind of effective spell, a subjective game that led her to struggle against appearances and to try to reach, within the wild heart of life, something unreachable, but also something that cannot be given up, for to give it up, in this case, would be to die. And Joana, we recall, refused to die, despite heading, in her unstoppable immobility, toward that "death-without-fear" she had chosen, ultimately, like a journey of renewal that, in the final analysis, she had to undertake.

Near the Wild Heart appeared undisguisedly as a very serious attempt at the introspective novel, having in its favor above all else a new syntactical process, matched by a spirit of inquiry and a restless instability, very much of our time.

One could not ask more from a debuting author. A well-received debut, then, that allowed us to expect more definitive results from future experiments that the novelist of course would offer us, and for which there would be no lack of encouragement from our most authoritative critics.

And other experiments were to come. *The Chandelier* arrived, which, though received with praise, didn't have the same impact as the first book. In *The Chandelier*, the author decided to push on with the development of that new syntax, as if to lend to it the character of a thesis. That syntax she imposed upon it that, if deepened, might have resulted in a spontaneous philosophy. One got the impression that the author was wanting to establish her personality in style or phrase. It was a show of strength performed with that game of multiple images, abstract or concrete, alternating or interrupted, that emerged from her sentences, adorning them with her reflections. But all that still didn't have the power to let us reach a more general conclusion, one that was more fully satisfactory regarding the progression of life beyond some verbal sleight-of-hand, which seemed to be the limit of the author's intention. *The Chandelier* had really been a book for which the most appropriate verdict actually was the one it received—a kind of suspension of judgment. A suspension of judgment that did not preclude a well-founded fear of the abuse of those talents, deployed more as an end in themselves rather than as a means, to the detriment of her vision and to the complexity of the literary psychology of our time, which can no longer be restricted to a pure question of phraseology. A question, after all, that ends up leading nowhere.

But the litmus test was not in this second novel. It would come in what was to follow. After a long interval came *The Besieged City* (published by "A Noite," Rio), which was written in Switzerland.

What's clear is that this new book can no longer be judged as an attempt. For Clarice Lispector, the experimental phase has passed. We must look at it, therefore, as a completed work.

Does the book really open new possibilities for the Brazilian novel? Does its way with syntax really constitute in fact the missing measure that would establish firmly the place of the woman in our literary world?

If the method of suggestive description endures, with great opportunities to show what it can do, it doesn't quite give us an impression of fullness, of something defined, real. The feeling of obscurity, of indeterminacy, persists.

The Besieged City is a grueling novel to read. It requires tremendous effort to get through it. And the worst thing is that, having finished it, we don't feel the effort was worth it. On the one hand, if a sensibility emerges that is very attentive to the free movements of Lucrécia Neves's subconscious, to her thoughts and feelings, we aren't given, on the other hand, an impression of overarching meaning. Each mental or emotional incident that is analyzed—Lucrécia at her mirror, her conversation with Perseu Maria, her dreams of marriage, her attitude toward the husband who turns up one day, the outsider Mateus, etc.—is emotionally relevant in and of itself and can be glimpsed outside the center from which it radiates, which, everything leads us to believe, must be São Geraldo.

São Geraldo, the city invaded by progress, but which as a township rises up to a life of its own, becoming mostly a refuge for certain lives that have refused the new era, seems to be the *point de repère* for the whole story. Lucrécia Neves and the horses live their lives there, too, representing the two races of builders that started the tradition of the future metropolis, as the novelist says, and that could have appeared on its coat of arms.

But Lucrécia Neves had her own problems. And the horses, if they existed, if they were worth anything, lived in relation to her, to give birth to her fear in the shadows of her room, so much so that she begins to see things as a horse sees them. And the book, in fact, is full of equine images and references. They're not just the "foals, ponies, sorrels, long mares, hard hooves—a horse's cold and dark head—hooves beating, muzzles foaming rising toward the air in rage and grumbling" that advance and halt at the highest point of the hill, their heads dominating the township, to let out a long neigh. It's Lucrécia herself, who, when worked up, starts kicking with one of her hind legs at her absent tail. Who sometimes sees herself as an animal would see a house: no thought going beyond the house. Such was the intimacy without contact that she experienced when facing the horses, etc.

Moreover, Lucrécia Neves was beset by all kinds of revelations. These often appeared to her in dreams. The fantastic dreams she dreamt, with herds of mares sleepwalking out of the sewers, as well as ants, rats, wasps, pink bats. Here is a dream, as the novelist describes it and that gives a good idea of what the book is like, full of similar passages: "What the girl was seeing in her sleep was opening her senses as a house opens at dawn. The silence was funereal, tranquil, a slow alarm that couldn't be rushed. The dream was this: to be alarmed and slow. And also to look at the big things that were coming out from the tops of the houses just as you'd see yourself differently in someone else's mirror: twisted in a passive, monstrous expression. But the girl's monotonous joy was carrying on beneath the noise of the currents. The dream was unfolding as if the earth weren't round but flat and infinite, and thus there was time. The second floor was keeping her in the air. She was breathing herself out. The mirror of the room. But the girl turned her head to the side. Her heart kept beating in the premises. Then the mirror woke her."

And "discoveries" like this continue through the entire book. Now it's Lucrécia Neves's dream, later it's the dawn in her room that's described to us with the imagistic richness characteristic of Clarice Lispector's process, but with no apparent meaning, merely justifying a certain morbid taste for a phrase for the phrase's sake.

Everything that the novel offers—its lyrical power, the development of Lucrécia Neves's individual consciousness, the interspersed references to other beings and incidents without greater importance, etc.—fails to go beyond whatever verbal worth it might have. Everything is worthwhile in the eyes of this novelist, but she's susceptible to lacking discriminating taste. And the result is that the work circles around a life and a drama without managing to lend them more than a simulation of a novel.

TEMÍSTOCLES LINHARES

Esteemed Mr. X,

I came across your review of a book *The Besieged City*, God only knows from when, since the clipping isn't dated. Your review is pointed and well-done. You said so many true and well-expressed things that resonated in me—so that for a long time it didn't occur to me to add either to them or to myself other truths that are important in the same way. It so happens that you are or aren't to blame for not being aware of these other truths. I know that the average reader can only be aware of things that are complete, that are apparent. What astonishes me—and this is certainly my own fault—is that the higher purposes of my book should escape a critic. Does this mean I couldn't bring to the fore the book's intentions? Or were the critic's eyes clouded for other reasons, not my own? People speak, or rather, used to speak, so much about my "words," about my "phrases." As if they were verbal. Yet not one, not a single one, of the words in the book was—a game. Each of them essentially meant some thing. I still think of my words as being naked. As for the book's "intention," I didn't believe it was lost, in a critic's eyes, through the development of the narrative. I still feel that "intention" running through all the pages, in a thread perhaps fragile as I wished, but continuous and all the way to the end. I believe that all of Lucrécia Neves's problems are relative to that thread. What did I mean to say through Lucrécia—a character without the weapons of intelligence, who aspires, nonetheless, to that kind of spiritual integrity a horse has, who doesn't "share" what it sees, who has no mental or "vocabular vision" of things, who feels no need to complete impression with expression—the horse in which there is the miracle that the impression is total—so *real*—that in it impression already is expression. I really thought I'd suggested that Lucrécia Neves's true story was independent of her own personal story. The struggle to reach reality—that's the main objective of this creature who tries, in every way, to cling to whatever exists by means of a total vision of things. I meant to make clear too the way vision—the way of seeing, the viewpoint—alters reality, constructing it. A house is not only constructed with stones, cement etc. A man's way of looking constructs it too. The way of looking gives the appearance to reality. When I say that Lucrécia Neves constructs the city of São Geraldo and gives it a tradition, this is somehow clear to me. When I say that, at that time of a city being born, each gaze was making new extensions, new realities emerge—this is so clear to me. Tradition, the past of a culture—what is that besides a way of seeing that is handed down to us?

I thought I'd given Lucrécia Neves just the role of "one of the people" who built the city, allowing her the minimum individuality necessary for a being to be herself. Lucrécia Neves's particular problems, as you say, seem to me just the necessary ground for that collective construction. It seems so clear to me. One of the most intense aspirations of the spirit is to dominate exterior reality through the spirit. Lucrécia doesn't manage to do this—so she "clings" to that reality, takes as her own life the wider life of the world.

It's not apparent to me that all these intimate movements of the book, as well as others that complement them—were drowned by what you call the "spell of the phrase." Ever since my first book, moreover, there's been talk about my "phrases." Do not doubt, however, that I wanted—and reached, by God—some thing through them, and not the phrases themselves.

To call "verbalism" a painful desire to bring words as close as possible to feeling—that is what astonishes me. And what reveals to me the possible distance that exists between what is given and what is received ... But I know that what I gave was received. San Tiago Dantas, when he first read the book, was shocked: he told me I had "fallen." Later, on a sleepless night, he decided to reread it. And he told me astonished: but this is your best book. It wasn't, but I appreciated the deep understanding he had of Lucrécia Neves and the horses of São Geraldo. No, you didn't "bury" the book, sir: you too "constructed" it. If you'll excuse the word, like one of the horses of São Geraldo.

CLARICE LISPECTOR

Acknowledgments

The translator and the editor would like to thank the following people for their valuable suggestions regarding the trickier aspects of Clarice Lispector's diction and syntax: Schneider Carpeggiani, Pedro Corrêa do Lago, Flavio Goldman, Eduardo Heck de Sá, Ananda Lima, Michele Nascimento-Kettner, José Luiz Passos, Lis Veras, and Paulo Werneck.